I0725244

The Preacher

His Searchers

Book 3

By

Ronna M. Bacon

Copyright © 2022 Ronna M. Bacon
ISBN 978-1-989699-87-4

Hebrews 13:5

Let your conduct be without covetousness; be content with such things as you have. For He Himself has said, "I will never leave you nor forsake you."

Deuteronomy 31:6
"Be strong and of good courage, do not fear nor be afraid of them; for the LORD your God, He is the One who goes with you. He will not leave you nor forsake you."

NKJV

Table of Contents

The early summer air was hot and heavy with humidity. It felt stagnant from the lack of any breeze or wind or any air movement. It was the type of day that developed thunderstorms, sometimes violent, and on occasion, tornadoes.

Rogan Fitzgerald stood at the window in his office. He sighed before he reached an arm to wipe away the sweat beading on his forehead. He hated days like this, preferring the cooler days of spring or fall. He turned to study his office in the mission that he ran. Nodding, Rogan moved to tidy up his desk and lock away what he needed to. His desk locked in turn, he headed for the door and then shut and locked it behind him. It wasn't quitting time yet, but he always headed into the mission and then the surrounding area at the end of the day, just as he did at the beginning of the day. Rogan felt it necessary, to assess the people of the street and those who were low income that needed what help he provided.

Moving quietly among the people who had gathered in the mission great room, Rogan grinned at the comments sent his way. He enjoyed his work, helping those in need. As a minister, he had been offered a large church in a nearby town, but had refused. That was not where God had wanted him, and that fact had been clearly impressed on him.

Rogan stood for a moment, his eyes roving over the room before he headed towards the kitchen area. It would soon be time to head home for the night

—

himself. However, it was only late afternoon and it would be time to feed those around him. Rogan was concerned about those very people, making sure that they had a warm meal before they headed home or to the shelter or even to the derelict buildings some called home.

Pausing at a doorway, Rogan frowned before he leaned a shoulder against the doorframe and stood, one leg crossed over the other, his hands jammed into his pockets. He watched the young lady, around his age he thought, as she sat cross legged on the floor, a toddler on her legs, surrounded by at least six other small children. He listened as she read a story to them, her low melodious voice soothing the worries that he had been carrying. Rogan frowned for a moment before her name came to him.

Tate Benner was new to the area and had been staying in the shelter for a few days until she could find an apartment. He had talked briefly with her, not finding out much information from her. That concerned him to a certain degree, but he understood that came with the territory. The late afternoon sun shone on her dark auburn hair, bringing out the red highlights. He knew that her green eyes held depths that he felt he could drown in. His eyelids dropped over his dark gray eyes, hiding his emotions, before he ran his hand through his dark blond curls.

Rogan moved on, heading for the kitchen to see what he could do to help. Smiles and calls greeted him as he moved through the building. He laughed and waved and then paused, to turn once more to look behind him, staring at the doorway to the room where he had just stood. He shook his head, feeling a sense of doom and danger approaching. Rogan had learned not to ignore those feelings. Only, this time? He had no idea why he felt like he did or who else would be involved.

Tate had raised her head slightly as she heard Rogan moving away. She sighed even as she continued to read. She needed to find that apartment and get moved into it. That was proving more difficult than she thought. Her online work had continued even as she lived in the shelter, using the internet there to do that. Tate just wanted her own place. She lived in fear, hearing the footsteps that followed her as she walked through town and through the stores that she frequented. Only, Tate had no idea who it was. She had fled from town to town since she finished her college course in writing and literacy.

Rising at last, Tate made her way towards the kitchen as well. She didn't have to offer to help but she always did. It was the least that she felt she could do, to help those who were serving. It was the way that she had been raised, to serve others. Her parents had explained that was what God expected of them, to be His hands and feet on earth. Tate had questioned her mother at the time as she was not yet a teenager but she had watched her parents and then just followed their example. To lose her father in the house fire as she had? That had almost destroyed her mother. She had been in her second year of college when the fire happened. She just didn't understand why her father had not made it out. Refusing to speak with the investigators when they questioned her years later as a follow up, Tate had simply returned to her studies and then moved from town to town, running

—

from the truth, she knew. Only she didn't know that she wanted to know the truth.

Rogan spoke from beside her, causing her to jump in surprise.

"Sorry." He grinned at her, earning himself a frown in return. "I don't think that you heard me. You were deep in thought."

"Deep in memories is more like it." Tate sighed once more, feeling safe beside Rogan. Only she couldn't understand that. She looked up at him. She was tall for a lady but he was well over six foot. "Do you need help with anything?"

"Tell me again, Tate. What is your occupation?" Rogan didn't look directly at her, but caught her slight start.

"I work online as a proofreader for a Christian publisher. I have done secretarial work in the past. I shouldn't be staying here. I have work but not a home."

Rogan wondered at the sadness that crept across her face.

"Then, you're who I need. I am looking for a secretary. Care to help?" He grinned at her again.

"You're serious?" Tate remembered to snap her mouth closed. "Okay. I guess. When?"

"Today's Wednesday. How about Monday?" Rogan tilted his head to watch her face. "Your apartment?"

"I get it on the weekend." Rogan sighed. "It's furnished, but I need to shop for essentials and food."

"Not a problem, Tate. I have friends whose wives will help you. They know what it's like to be in danger."

"Who said I was in any danger?" Tate stared at him, wondering that he had figured it out.

"God told me that you were." Rogan's hand on her arm drew her to the outdoors. "I would like to help you, Tate, if you will let me. And my friends, who had been through danger and life-threatening adventures, would join us in that."

Tate blinked rapidly, her tears blinding her for a moment. She couldn't understand why but God, this is You. You have brought him into my life. Maybe now I can stop running and face whoever it is.

A sudden popping sound had Rogan spinning and then leaping for Tate, intending to take her to the ground and protect her. Only he didn't reach her in time. He landed hard on the ground beside her, horror on his face as he saw the blood on her shoulder. Rogan reached for her, scooping her into his arms and running for the building, hearing the popping sounds behind him, knowing that they were still under fire from an unknown assailant.

The door slammed open and he kicked it closed behind him, heading for the room that they had set up as a sick room. The cook, Sandy, stared at him and then was running towards that room, even as one of the helpers reached for the mission phone and called for help.

Rogan gently laid Tate down, reaching for the towels that Sandy has handing him.

"Rogan? What happened? What is going on?" Sandy was in shock and her bewildered voice sounded loud in the sudden silence.

"Tate was shot. I didn't see who. We need to call it in."

"Brenna's taken care of that. Here, step back. Let me." Sandy had been a nurse in her early years before retiring from burnout. "I'll take care of her. You need to talk to the residents here."

Rogan nodded, not sure what to say or even how to phrase it. He stood, his eyes on Tate, worry on his face, and an unreadable look in his eyes. He looked at the ceiling, praying for his friend, asking that her life be spared and that she healed quickly. Rogan also prayed for the emergency responders, turning as he heard the sirens, to head for the living area and the residents, meeting the paramedics and an officer on their way in. He simply pointed to where Tate lay.

Chapter 2

Rogan stood in the hallway, watching as the paramedics worked to stem the flow of blood and then assess Tate. He was afraid for his new friend, afraid that she would die. He had no idea who her next of kin were and turned as a hand touched his shoulder.

"Rogan?"   The patrol officer who had responded, David Johns, motioned him away. "What happened?"

"I really don't know. Tate and I were outside talking. I had asked her to come work for the mission as my secretary. Then there were popping noises and she was down." Rogan was worried, haunted by the sight of blood on Tate. He stared down at his hands, which he had not been able to clean as yet, staring at Tate's blood.

David drew in a sharp breath and then shoved Rogan towards the washroom on the floor. He turned on the water as hot as he could and then stared as Rogan just stood there in shock.

"Rogan? Here. Let's get you cleaned up as best we can." David finally reached for Rogan's hands and then the soap, shoving them into the stream of water.

Rogan shook his head, coming back to the present, scrubbing at his hands to clean them as best

---

he could. He reached for the towel, rubbing his hands dry, a puzzled look on his face.

"Why, David? Why Tate?"

"That's what we're looking at. How well do you know her? I mean, you did offer her work." David turned Rogan back towards the outside, watching as the paramedic rig pulled away.

"She's been living here until her apartment opens up. That is Monday. She doesn't have much more than what can fit into her luggage. That's what she said just before she was shot. I was going to round up friends to help her." Rogan blew out a breath. Lord, please? Heal my new friend. Let us figure out what has happened.

"The guys will work on it. What else?"

Rogan shook his head, not sure what to say.

"She just said that she had been moving from town to town since she finished college. She does proofreading on line. Her father is dead. I don't know about her mother. I'm sorry, David. I don't know much else."

"That's okay. We'll work on that. Now, you need to speak with your people. They're waiting for you." David glanced behind them, to see the residents waiting for Rogan.

"I know. I just don't know what to say." Rogan turned to face the building, his eyes tracing over the men, women, and children who stood waiting for him. He began to pray once more, asking for God to speak through him. He walked towards his family, as he called them, stopping to speak with

—

each one, taking the hugs and the handshakes, lifting the little ones up in his arms.

David watched him before he turned once more. This was frustrating, he thought. No one had seen anyone. He knew fellow officers were canvassing the area but none of them expected to find the culprit.

Standing in the Emergency Room waiting room, Rogan stared around. He felt lost. He had been there before for friends and residents who had been hurt. This time, though, it felt different. This time it was a lady who he was interested in, although he didn't acknowledge that to himself. Rogan walked through the doors to the examination rooms, following the nurse who had come to find him. It disturbed him that Tate had no next of kin. He sighed, knowing that he would ask to be put down as such, just on a temporary basis until Tate could make a decision as to who she wanted to do that.

The nurse threw a glance at Rogan, compassion in her glance. Rogan was well known and well liked by the staff at the hospital. He was willing to step in and help wherever he could.

"Right in there, Rogan. John Thomas will be in shortly."

Rogan nodded before he looked behind. Uncertainty was in his bearing, totally unlike him. He was a confident man who was sure of his movements. This time? It was different. Tate had no idea why but he prayed for his new friend. His sneakers squeaked slightly on the tiled floor as he moved toward the bed.

His hands resting on the bedrail, Rogan stared at the equipment surrounding the stretcher. He had studied just such equipment many times before. This time, it felt different. He felt his phone vibrating and ignored it. Tate was the important one right now.

His hand rested gently on her cheek as her eyes flickered. She was rousing and he had to prepare himself to tell her what happened. Quiet footsteps approached and stopped beside him.

David watched Rogan, seeing the distress that his friend was feeling. He then turned his attention to Tate, finding her somewhat alert and moving restlessly.

"Tate?" Rogan's voice caught her attention.

"Rogan? Where am I? I hurt." She sighed, her eyes sliding closed against the pain.

"You're in the hospital, Tate. You were shot."

"Shot?" Her eyes sprang open as she frantically stared up at him. "Shot? Not me!" She tried to raise herself up, falling back with pain, a hand reaching for her arm and shoulder.

"Yes, you." Rogan hesitated a moment before he reached to touch her arm, resting his hand on it.

"He found me, did he?" Rogan stared around her, eyes suddenly seeing David. Fear shot through her. "Who are you?"

"I'm David Johns, the patrol officer who responded. I just needed to ask you some questions." He frowned at the look that covered her face, a sudden look of fear. "Tate, may I call you that?" At her nod, he studied her once more. "What happened? Who would be after you?"

"Me? After me? I don't know. As far as I know, I don't have any enemies. I've moved around, just because I couldn't settle down in any town. None felt like home, until here. Why would you ask that?"

"Because the trajectory of the shots was right to where you were standing. Not at Rogan. Not at anyone else. Just you. So again, who is after you?"

Chapter 3

Sighing to herself and then rolling to her good side away from Rogan, Tate tucked the covers up around her neck and close her eyes. Just maybe, she thought, if I can't see the two men, they'll disappear. She sighed once more, hearing their restlessness as they both shifted their weight from foot to foot.

"I don't know why." She rolled back, momentarily closing her eyes against the pain from her arm. "Where did I get hurt?"

"Your shoulder. The bullet caused a deep crease." Rogan studied her, a slight smile crossing his face. "Now, behave, Tate. David does need to speak with you. I'll leave and let him."

Tate's good hand shot out and grabbed at his arm, stopping him in his tracks. She shook with fear, not from David or even Rogan. Just why that was? She couldn't say. The only thing that Tate knew was that she did not want Rogan walking away from her. Not then. Not ever. That thought caused her to pause, her hand tightening on his arm. She felt his eyes on her and shook briefly before she looked at David.

"What do you need to know?"

David stared at her for a moment, not quite sure what he had just witnessed. He then in turn studied Rogan, finding Rogan staring in turn at Tate, a look on his face that was hard to describe.

———

"Just what can you tell me? Have you been followed? Receive any unwanted attention, packages, mail?" He grinned at her as she frowned at him. He could almost hear her brain working.

"I don't think so. At least, I didn't take it as that. I had the odd bouquet of flowers delivered to me without a card but that was a couple of years ago and not in this town. I've only been here a couple of weeks at the most." Tate's head went back as her eyes closed. She struggled to remember, to stay alert, but fatigue and pain and shock did their work and she slept.

"I think that you lost her, David." Rogan grinned. "Can we take this up later?"

"It looks as if we will have to. Where are you planning on taking her? Back to the shelter?" David tucked his notepad and pen back into his uniform shirt.

Rogan shook his head.

"That won't work. I don't have a nurse there overnight." Rogan bit at his lip, not sure where to take her.

"Take her to your home. Your sister's there for the next couple of days, isn't she?"

Rogan nodded. Rori was indeed visiting. God, You were planning ahead. She's a nurse and that works out well. By Monday, hopefully, Tate will be healed enough to manage in her own apartment. Only, I worry about that. I don't want her on her own.

A couple of hours later, Rori watched with a frown on her face as her brother carried Tate towards his front door. Rogan had gathered Tate into his arms, despite her protest that she could walk, and simply shook his head. His raised foot gave a gentle shove to the door and it shut quietly. Tate's belongings were in his trunk, he had slipped away and gathered them. The staff had nodded, knowing as did Rogan that they were not equipped to care for her, not at that stage of her injury.

"Rogan? What is going on? Who is this?" Rori shut the carved wooden door behind her and then followed Rogan as he headed for the living room.

"This is Tate Benner, Rori. She was shot earlier at the mission. I couldn't leave her there." Rogan felt like he was pleading with his younger sister to understand. They had a close relationship, and he just prayed that she would.

"Of course, you couldn't. Thank the good Lord that I'm here for the next few days." Rori slipped to a sitting position on the coffee table, her eyes on Tate. Finding Tate watching her, a shuttered look on her face amid the look of pain, Rori grinned. "Hi. I'm Rori, Rogan's sister. You're safe here for now."

Tate felt relieved, for now she thought.

"Thank you. I hate to put you in danger, though." Tate's head went back on the couch as her eyes closed.

Rogan stood for a moment, having dropped her bags into the other spare room, before he moved towards the kitchen. He had been warned that he

---

needed to get some food into Tate, light food or liquid he had been told. Rogan knew that he had soup in the fridge and reached for it. Dumping it into a sauce pan, he set it to heat and then reached for bread. He turned to the door and then reached for the toaster. Toast, he thought, rather than a sandwich. Loading a tray with the mugs of soup, the plate of toast, crackers, spoons, and their cups of tea, Rogan hesitated, bowing his head. He felt out of place right now and only his Heavenly Father could help. He stood for a moment in the hallway, listening to Rori's quiet comments and gentle laugh as she spoke with Tate. Tate's responses had been brief to start with but were getting longer. Smiling to himself, Rogan looked up. His sister always had a way with her to draw people out. As a nurse, that trait helped her to understand her patients' needs. He was so glad that she was moving back to their town, taking up employment as a visiting nurse.

Rori looked around as she heard Rogan's quiet footsteps and stood to help him sort out their food. She sat in his chair, smirking at him as he frowned for a moment before he sat beside Tate on the couch. A quick blessing on their food and they were eating.

Tate's glance shifted between the siblings, her eyes watchful. She had been an only child, her father, her father killed in a fire when she was young and she had no recollection of him. Her mother had struggled to make ends meet and one day, just walked away from it all, leaving Tate devastated. She was in her last year of her studies at that point. She had not understood at all why her mother had done that. She had had no contact with her parent since then, although at times she was certain that she had seen her mom around her.

Chapter 4

Tate's sleep was restless and dream filled. Nightmare filled, she decided in the early morning hours, was more like it. Visions of a gun pointing at her and firing at her dominated those dreams. She wept in her sleep, her voice calling in a low tone for help. Only no help seemed to be coming. Sitting up just as dawn was breaking, Tate awkwardly shoved pillows behind her and rested back on them. She stared at the window, hearing the sounds of the morning as the critters emerged from their nightly slumber. Sighing, she then raised her eyes to the ceiling, praying for this to have only been a bad nightmare, that she really hadn't been shot and was now at Rogan's home.

Turning her attention to the door, Tate finally rose and searched for clothing that would be easy to don. She gave a small smile. Rori had approached her the night before, asking if she could help her find clothes for the morning. Tate had been taken aback for a moment and then accepted.

Dressed, somewhat in her right mind, but determined to continue with her plans to move into her own apartment on Monday, Tate moved silently through the house, heading for the kitchen and tea. She desperately needed a cup of tea, she thought, seeking the comfort that would bring to her. With her cup in hand, she moved towards the back yard and then just stood on the deck, her face raised to the sky, as she prayed. There was a desperation in her prayer that morning, one that she could not understand.

The vibration of her phone startled her and Tate reached for it. She frowned as she pulled up the text message and then went pale. Her life had just taken another turn for the worst. The landlord of her new apartment had just sent a text, telling her that she was no longer a tenant, that he was refusing to rent to her. No lease had been signed, she thought. Tears clouded her eyes as she drew in a deep breath. *Now what, Lord? I still have to live at the shelter. Only my time there is over. I have surpassed what I can. Now to go apartment hunting once more and I certainly don't feel like it.* Tate sank down into a chair, her good hand covering her eyes as she struggled to control her tears.

Rogan stood for a moment in the kitchen before he too reached for a mug of tea and then headed for the back door. His steps stopped as he found Tate before he moved towards her, his mug on the table and then his hand resting on her head. He felt her jump before he began to pray for her.

Tate raised her head at long last, causing Rogan to draw in a deep breath at the devastation and hurt and despair on her face.

"Tate? What happened?"

Tate looked at him and then simply shoved her phone at him. Rogan caught it before it fell, not taking his eyes from her.

"Tate?"

"My apartment? I no longer have it. He's refusing to rent to me. Read the text."

—

Rogan kept his eyes on her, even as he heard quiet conversation floating out from the kitchen. David, he thought, is here and Rori is up. He looked down at the text, drawing in a deep breath as he read it.

"He did that? Oh, Tate, I am so sorry." Rogan looked at her, seeing the raw hurt in her eyes. "We'll find you a place. I can guarantee you that. A much better place."

"Why bother? I'll just move to another town. It's not the first time something like this has happened." Tate rubbed at the arm in the sling, pain increasing as her body tensed. She didn't hear David approach or hear Rori sit beside her. She jumped as Rori's arm came around her.

"Tate? We'll find you something. For now, I'm staying with Rogan, so that means you can too." Rori didn't have to look at her brother to know he was nodding in agreement. "But first, David's here. He just needs to speak with you. Rogan and I will leave you two on your own."

Tate's hands were out, gripping both Rogan's and Rori's. They could feel the fear that she was feeling in her grip.

"No, please, stay. David?" Tate shot him a look, seeing him hesitate and then nod. "They can stay?"

"They shouldn't, but I'll allow it. Only they can't say anything or react in any way or I'll have to remove them." David shared a look with Rogan and then Rori before he frowned at Tate. "Okay, Tate. What happened in the past?"

Tate looked up, shocked at his question, before she sank back against the chair. Her thoughts were tumbled and troubled. She gave a huge sigh and then blinked. No one had ever asked her that before.

"David? Why ask that?" Tate was genuinely puzzled.

"Because it was a deliberate attempt to kill you yesterday, if not seriously hurt you. You were the target. There has to be a reason. I understand that you have only been here in town for a couple of weeks." David watched carefully as she nodded. "So, it has to have been something from somewhere else that caused this."

"You're right. Let me just give a bit of background. My dad was killed in an fire when I was young. Mom struggled to raise me, leaving when I was just finishing college. I have no idea where she went to or why. Since then, I have moved from town to town, just trying to find somewhere I could settle down and have it feel like home. My mom rented an apartment for us. They had a house but I think she lost it when she couldn't pay the mortgage. At least, that's what she used to say. But I think the bank took it back. She always said that they didn't have insurance to cover the loss.

"But as to who did this? I have no idea. I wish I did. I'd track him down and confront him."

David looked stern at that.

"That is exactly what we don't want you to do. It could well mean your life. Or the lives of your friends." David smiled as she looked at him, her mouth open to protest that she had no friends. "You do have friends here, Tate. Rogan. Rori. Myself. Rogan's friends. They will all want to help you, that much I know."

Rogan chose that moment to speak up.

"David's right, Tate. My friend will help. The people at the shelter? They will look out for you. That's how they are and what they do."

Tate had turned to him, hope rising inside her that maybe, just maybe, she had found a place to fit in, to find friends, and to make a home. *God, is this You? Are You the One who brought me here, to this town, to these people? I need to find that hope and love that You tell me is out there. Thank you.*

"Then, all I can say is thank you." She turned to David. "What now?"

"What now? We look into your past, your parents, your acquaintances and friends. Your employer. Your landlords."

"Yeah, about that." Tate blinked rapidly for a moment. "The landlord here just refused me the apartment. Said he didn't want street trash living there. After assuring me that me living in the shelter for a couple of weeks was not a problem."

David frowned, before he reached for the phone she kept thrusting at him. He read the text and then asked her permission to forward it to himself. He recognized the name and knew that Tate had escaped the clutches of one of the worse men in town. Rogan's movement caught his attention and the two men exchanged glances, both nodding in relief.

"It is better that you don't live there, Tate." David looked at her with compassion. "You would not have known, but he is deep into crime. It is rumoured that he forces his tenants into crime. Only, no one has ever confirmed that."

Chapter 5

Tate moved around the kitchen, not really listening to the teasing that Rori was undergoing. David had left and in his place someone named Austin had appeared. He was apparently a friend of Rogan's but she didn't realize that he was a detective on the force.

Standing beside the counter, Rogan's hand came out to stop Tate, his eyes on her for a moment. *Lord, this is difficult with her. I can't understand how she feels but You do. Please be with my friend and protect her. Help Austin to determine what actually is going on. And something is, that much I know. Only I am afraid for her.*

"Rogan?" Tate's voice brought him back to the present and to the kitchen.

"Tate? What are we to do with you?" He watched her closely, seeing hope in her eyes.

"I don't know, Rogan. I really don't know. I can't put you and your family at risk. Staying here will do that. And besides, I can't stay here for long."

"No, you can't, Tate. I have an idea that I would like to speak with you about but first, we need to spend some time in deep prayer. Austin is here as my friend. But he is a detective on the force. Some of my friends are or were officers. They will help. I don't even have to ask them to know that."

"They would? I have never had friends like that." She blinked rapidly, thinking about how lonely she had felt all her life. Not now, though, she thought, surprised at that. She had friends who cared. Rogan and Rori for two.

"They would. Tomorrow is Saturday and we usually get together at one of their places for a meal. I would like it if you would come with me." Rogan gave an irrepressible grin at that.

Tate started to shake her head before she felt Rori's arm around her and turned to study her new friend.

"It would do you good, Tate. They have all had adventures, as we call it. Then you can talk to the ladies and see what they suggest. I can't make it, even though I'm asked." Rori shared a long look with Rogan, knowing somewhat how her brother thought. She herself would be moving out to her own place within the week. And just where would that leave Tate?

Late that night, Tate curled up on the couch, not willing to go to bed. She dreaded the dreams that she would have, dreams that she realized now had been haunting her sleep for years. Her shoulder was aching and sore but not quite as bad as it had been.

Rogan set a cup of tea down beside her before he dropped into his arm chair, his eyes closing for a moment. His emotions were all over the place and that didn't help him to make any rational decisions. At least, where Tate was concerned.

"Rogan? You should be in bed. You have a big day tomorrow, don't you?" Tate's voice was

---

quiet in the dimness of the living room, with just a couple of lights on. She had stared around it as she had sat, liking the simple furnishings and the earth-tone colours that Rogan had chosen.

"So should you. Sorry about today. I didn't know that so many people would walk through." A number of friends had walked through the house, worried about Tate and wanting to know where she was. They had not been surprised to see her with Rogan and Rori.

"It's okay. It's your home. I shouldn't be here." Tate snuggled deeper under the afghan. She yawned and then gave a small smile at Rogan's grin.

"They're concerned about you, Tate. They want to help and will. I know that I don't have a regular church as you would call it, but the mission is dear to many of my friends and they support it. I do have to go in to the shelter for a bit tomorrow. I always do, just to ensure everyone has what they need. I don't need to but I like to keep up on what is going on."

"Okay. That's not what I have come to expect from a minister. In my experience, they're not like that." Tate was lost to Rogan for a moment as she thought back on the churches that she had been involved in. "I'll find something to do. I need to go looking for an apartment." She looked up at Rogan as he gave a small sound. "Rogan?"

"Tate? There is something that I am praying through and would like to discuss with you." His hand went up as she opened her mouth. "Just think about this. I would offer you my name and home for now, until Austin can solve this. I just fear for you."

Tate's mouth opened and closed, shock her uppermost emotion. Did he really just ask that, Lord? She hesitated for a moment, knowing what her answer should be but she was reluctant to do that.

"Rogan? Are you sure? That's a big step. We don't know each other, not the way that we should." Tate could hear the gentle dong of the grandfather clock from the corner of the room.

"I am, Tate. I really am. I'm sure of what I am asking. I just don't know for sure that's the best step." He paused, his eyes on the floor. "Just pray about it. That's all I ask. If you say no, we'll find some other way to keep you alive." He stood, hesitated, and then walked away, to shut his bedroom door behind him. Rogan would not sleep that night, he knew. Instead, he would spend it in intercessory prayer for the lady who was becoming important to him. Sure, he thought, he hadn't known her for long but she had stirred something up in his heart that he had long hidden, the dream of a wife and family.

Tate stared after him, a hand covering her mouth, even as tears sparkled on her face. *Lord, is this You? Is this the plan that You have for me? I know Rogan would not offer this to just anyone. That's not him or his character. But how do I do this? I am dangerous, I know. And that might just mean his life.*

—

Chapter 6

The next morning, Rogan walked through the mission and spoke with each one. His laughter rang out, covering his worry about Tate. He stopped in the area where Tate had been shot, his eyes on the ground and then rising to look around. He could feel eyes on him and the danger that was arising too. He feared for his new friend. Tate had not been up when he had to leave and that had disappointeded him.

Tate had heard Rogan as he had left, standing at her window and staring out into the street. She was torn by what he had asked, needing to talk with someone, to seek counsel but not knowing who to speak with. Rori had watched her closely later, not knowing what was going on with her, but knowing that she was trying to make a decision.

"Tate? Let's head to the stores down town. You need to do something fun." Rori simply grinned at her. "We'll take care, Tate, and only do what you can handle. Rogan's at the mission, working through tomorrow's service, more than likely. It's what he does on Saturdays."

Tate stared at her and then shrugged as best she could.

"Sure. Why not? But I do have to look for an apartment."

"We'll do that. I know someone who would take you in for a few days."

"You do?" Tate felt hope rising within her. Maybe, just maybe, this had not been a mistake after all, coming to this town.

"I do. You can come live with me. I would like that. You're in need of my help and I need your help."

"My help? Just what would that be?"

"I need your friendship. In case you didn't pick it up, Rogan doesn't do what he did with you. He would have found somewhere else for you to stay. He's made a connection with you that I have not seen before."

"I see." Tate bit at her lip as she stared at the store front that Rori had parked in front of. "I guess that makes sense then, what he asked last night."

Rori locked her car and then approached Tate, a frown crossing her face briefly as she stared at the man who stood, his eyes on Tate.

"And that would be?" Rori waited before she sighed. She thought that she knew what Rogan would have asked. "He asked you to marry him, didn't he?"

Tate hesitated and then nodded.

"He did. I just don't want to have him hurt." Tate moved away from Rori, leaving the other lady staring after her before she ran to catch up with her.

"I know my brother or as best as anyone can. If he has offered you this, then he has prayed it through."

Tate nodded and then reached for a soft yellow sweater. She did need to replace some clothes, only she had an apartment to find first.

"Tate, I did mean it. You can stay with me for however long you need to."

"Thank you, Rori. I really appreciate that. I just don't want to put you in danger. That's why I can't go back to the shelter." Tate blinked rapidly for a moment, her emotions getting the best of her for a moment.

"We get that. Here, that sweater? It would be perfect on you." Rori nodded as Tate looked up. "I get that you haven't had many friends over the years, Tate. I understand. I want to be your friend, no matter what happens. God has brought us together."

An hour later, Tate slid into a booth in the local diner that Rori liked to frequent. She listened as Rori was greeted and then reached for the menu. She was hungry but needed to find something that she could eat with only one hand.

"It's okay, Tate. They'll find you something to eat that you can." Rori simply grinned at her and then looked past her, surprise on her face.

Tate jumped as a hand reached for hers and she looked up in fear. Her face softened as Rogan moved to sit beside her on the bench seat.

"Rogan? I thought that you were busy."

"I was, Tate, but I was told that you were downtown and that you needed me." He simply grinned as she frowned at him.

"You were? I guess." She shared a look with Rori, seeing Rori barely able to contain her amusement. "Rori?"

Rori shook her head, denying that she had called her brother. David slid down beside Rori, causing Tate to frown at him in turn.

"I'm the guilty one, Tate. I saw you two and just knew that Rogan needed to be here."

Tate stared among the three, bothered for a moment, before she relaxed. God, this is You. I know that. Thank you.

"Well, then, we eat. But how do we fill the rest of the day?"

As they walked along the sidewalk, Rogan reached for Tate's hand, not finding her resisting his clasp. Tate studied their hands and relaxed. Rogan made her feel safe and cherished, something that she hadn't had in years.

"Tate? We need to talk. There is an urgency that I became aware of this morning." Rogan bit at his lower lip, not seeing the man watching them.

"I see. Then, I guess we must. How do we go about getting what we need?" Tate felt the slight hesitation in Rogan's steps and then the tightening of his hand on hers.

"I took steps yesterday to obtain the license, not sure if we would ever need it. A friend helped out. I also have another friend whose father is a pastor. He would marry us." Rogan drew her to a shop. "Here, let's go in here. Rori will help."

Tate stared up at him, wondering at his height. Over six foot for sure, she thought. And a gentle man who will protect me. Her gaze drifted past him to the man who had been following her. She frowned for a moment, thinking that she should know him, but not sure if she even did.

Chapter 7

Tate moved through the dresses, her hand gently touching them. Rori followed, a soft smile on her face. *God, this is You. I know it is. Tate needs healing in so many ways. Help her to reach out to touch the garment's hem and receive all that healing.*

Drawing in a soft breath, Tate stared at a dress. It was simple in design, with a lace overdress and just cap sleeves. It would work, she decided, as she reached for the price tag. And it was on sale, well within her means.

"Tate, that is just so you!" Rori hugged her, being mindful of her wound. "Do you want to try it on?"

"No, I don't think so. The only thing is the bandage. How do we hide that?" Tate chewed at her lip.

The saleslady had approached, with a small cape-like garment in her hands.

"This would work. It's lace but it goes with the dress. You could wear it for the photos."

Tate fingered it and nodded, her emotions getting the best of her for a moment.

The man who had been watching Tate sighed to himself. He needed to speak with Tate, having finally tracked her down. He had information that he needed to confirm and clarify with her. This situation she

---

37

was now in? He had tried to reach her to prevent it, but hadn't been able to.

Rogan simply reached to hug Tate, mouthing a thank you to his sister. Rori blinked back her own tears. This is not how she ever expected her brother to marry. Now, she was on a mission to find their parents and younger brother. They were in town, somewhere, she knew.

"I'll find Mom and Dad and Reece." She turned and walked away, David keeping steps with her. "David? How safe are they really?"

David shrugged. "I don't know. We really don't have a lot of information."

"You're saying then that they are at risk and we can't do anything about it."

"Not at the moment." He glanced behind him, troubled about his friend.

Rogan turned late that afternoon, watching as Tate walked across his parents' living room towards him. He had never expected this, he thought. His parents had been shocked, he thought, when he talked with them. His mother had simply hugged him. His father had stood, hands on his shoulders and watched him closely. Reuben had nodded and then hugged his son, holding on a bit longer than he would have normally. Rosa had as well, a mom prayer whispered in his ears.

Reece had been vocal, asking questions that Rogan could not answer before he had simply prayed with his brother. This was so Rogan, he thought. She must be very special for him to do this.

———

Tate had met his family briefly, Rori beside her, an arm around Tate. She had been so uncertain as to what their reaction would be. To be welcomed as she had been was not what she had expected.

Hours later, Rogan wandered his home, his thoughts muddled. To say that he was a married man now, newly married, still astonished him. Tate, he knew, was out on the back deck, needing some alone time. He headed that way, stopping to grab mugs of tea for them. Lights had been dimmed in the house, leaving just a slight glow through the windows.

Tate looked up as Rogan approached, taking the mug that he was handing her. He sat beside her on the love seat, an arm around her to draw her close to him. She stiffened for a moment before she relaxed against him. *I've come home, haven't I, Lord? This is where You want me? I am so afraid though of what is to come. I feel a sense of impending doom and only You can walk us through that.*

"You okay?" Rogan's voice was low.

"I guess. You?" Tate struggled to see his face in the dark, lit only by solar lights.

"I am. Thank you, Tate, for agreeing to marry me. I'll do my best to keep you safe." He sighed. "And we have church tomorrow."

"We do. How do we explain us?" Tate struggled to come up with words or a plan to do just that.

Rogan shrugged. "We won't have to. Word will have gotten around. My people will accept up, I know that, and they will watch out for you. It's a given. It's what they do for me and now that you're my family, they'll do that for you."

"They will? Okay, I guess." Tate shifted restlessly, her wound burning and hurting. "What about your friends?"

Rogan chuckled, drawing an inaudible sound from Tate.

"It's okay, Tate. My close friends have had what we call adventures. We need to connect with them and let you hear their stories. Some of them married quickly just like we did. They are deeply in love and happy."

"Is that what will happen with us?" Tate stared up at him, finding his gaze on her.

"Only God knows that, Tate, my love. But that is my prayer. That we do fall in love and spend our life here together." His emotions were on his face, showing her his heart.

Tate drew in a deep breath, not realizing how open her own face was. This is it, isn't it, Lord?

Chapter 8

Three days later, Tate wandered the backyard of her new home. She should be working but had contacted her employer for a leave of absence for a couple of weeks. She needed that, she had told him, explaining what had happened. He had been concerned about her and just told her to finish the book that she was proofreading, take some time, and then call him. Tate was one of the best proofreaders that they had, he assured her. She had never taken any time off and should have.

She turned as she heard a throat being cleared and frowned. She didn't know the man who stood in front of her and felt fear flowing through her.

"I'm sorry, Tate. I didn't mean to startle you." The man held out a business card. "I'm a private investigator who was tasked with finding you."

"You were? Who would do that?"

"A relative who is concerned about you. Not your mother. But a cousin of your father."

"A cousin? I'm afraid I don't understand." Tate stood her ground, ready to turn and run if she had to.

"A cousin. I have verified it all." He held up an envelope. "I'll leave this for you. My business card is inside as well. Go over it with your husband and the police. They can contact me." He paused, his eyes troubled. "You need to be very careful, Tate. Someone wants you dead. Only I could not determine who or why."

Tate stared at him, a puzzled frown on her face. She felt like she should know him. Only she didn't think that she did.

"How did you find me?" Her voice was barely above a whisper, fear evident in it.

"It wasn't hard, Tate. You are a very attractive lady who is hard to forget. I have trailed you from town to town for the last year." He pointed at the envelope. "The evidence you need is there. Go through it. It will go harder with you now that you are married. The people responsible will go after him to get to you."

"I don't understand why. I don't remember Mom talking about any relatives."

"They cut your father out of their lives when your parents married. The reasons are in that package." The man hesitated and then shaking his head, disappeared around the house.

Tate stood, her hand gripping the envelope before she spun in a circle, searching for whoever it was that was watching her and then ran for the house, slamming the backdoor and locking it behind her. The envelope was dropped to the table as she almost ran to the front door, her hand on the lock to ensure that it was indeed engaged. Tate was afraid, more afraid than she had ever been.

Reaching for her phone, she hesitated, not wanting to disturb Rogan, even though he had told her to. She jumped as it chimed, dropping it to the counter before she swiped the screen and brought up a text message. Austin, the detective, was in the area. Could he speak with her? And yes, Rogan was on his way home at Austin's request.

Rogan's sneakers hit the tray in the front clothes cupboard before he moved rapidly through the house, looking for his bride. He didn't hesitate as he found her standing in the kitchen, staring at the tabletop. He simply moved in and wrapped her into a tight hug.

Tate had jumped as she heard the soft footsteps and then jumped even more as she felt arms around her. She struggled for a moment until she heard his softly whispered prayer and relaxed against him. Her good hand grasped at his.

Austin stood watching the couple. He had not expected Rogan to take the step that he had, but then again, he should have. It was the character of the man who he was beginning to know as a friend. He didn't want to be here, but he had no choice. He had been told that he needed to talk with Tate and that Rogan would need to be there. Austin had just stared at the chief of detectives before he nodded. Another friend, he thought. How many more would go through this?

Rogan looked up at that point, seeing Austin and then sliding out a chair to make Tate sit. He couldn't escape her hand though. She just refused to let go of him.

Austin frowned before he moved to the cupboard. Making his coffee and their tea, he mulled over what he needed to say. The couple behind him

---

weren't talking. Rogan moved towards the fridge, looking at the time. It was lunch time and they needed to eat. Sandwiches were quickly made and on a plate on the table before the two men sat, heads bowing for the blessing.

Tate nibbled at her sandwich, not wanting to eat, her stomach roiling with fear, but knowing that she had to, at some point. Rogan watched her carefully, his eyes moving to the envelope at times, not quite sure what had happened that morning. But something had. Of that, he was sure.

Austin helped to clear away the remnants of their meal, his eyes flickering between Rogan and Tate. Tate didn't move, her eyes on the envelope once more. It scared her, Austin could see. Just where had it come from, he wondered?

"Tate?" Rogan's arm came around his bride. "Let me pray for us and then we'll talk about that envelope."

Tate turned to stare at him, and he drew in a deep breath at the stark terror in her eyes. What had happened that afternoon to cause that, he wondered?

Chapter 9

Raising his head, Austin opened his mouth to speak and then clapped it shut. He needed to wait, he decided. What was in that envelope that scared Tate so much? That was what he wondered.

"Tate? Talk to me. Tell me what happened?" Rogan was desperate to find out what had gone on that day.

"Some man appeared this morning. He gave me that. He said that he was a private investigator." Tate turned to Austin, knowing that he was a detective. "He said his card was in the envelope. I haven't looked at it. Not a peek. I just couldn't. It scares me."

"What did he say about it?" Austin waited patiently.

"Just that it was about my family. A cousin of my father was looking for me and had hired him. I don't remember any of Dad's family. That man said that Dad's family walked away from him when he and Mom married."

"Okay. Let me look through it and then we can talk about it." Austin reached for the envelope, pulling on latex gloves before he did so. He carefully opened the clip holding it closed and pulled out all the paperwork.

—

Tate and Rogan watched closely as he did so, not sure what to expect. Rogan's arm stayed around her, tightening as he found her shuddering more and more. He knew that fear was rising within her and he wanted to remove that, if he could. Only he couldn't. Not at present.

Austin looked up at long last, his eyes troubled as were his thoughts. He had no idea who this investigator was, but he would be looked into, that was a given. He didn't know what to make of the material either.

"Tate, just for the record. You don't know this man?" She shook her head as he watched her closely. "And you have no idea of what was in this?"

"Absolutely not. I have never seen him. And I know nothing about my father's family. And not much more about Mom's. Why?"

"He has given a lot of information on your families, particularly your father's. I just needed to know what you did remember."

Tate shrugged, feeling Rogan's arm tighten around her.

"Can I see that?"

Austin nodded.

"It was given to you. If you would, I would like a copy of it."

Rogan was on his feet, heading for his office, returning with copies of the material.

"I would suggest that you take the original." He paused at the look on Tate's face. "Or not. We can keep the original. I'll lock it away and we can work from copies." Rogan knew that he had made the right decision and simply hugged her.

"We can do that. If we need the original, we can always ask for that."

The three worked away on the material, Tate surprised and shocked at what she was reading. She rose to pace, a hand rubbing at her shoulder. The wound was healing quicker than the surgeon had thought. She had been there earlier that morning for an assessment. He had sat back, smiled, and told her that the wound had been just through the top of the muscle. He didn't see any reason why she wouldn't completely recover.

Rogan watched her for a moment and then glanced at the clock. He groaned. He had a conference call that he had to make and that time was then. He rose as well, leaving Austin on his own, deep into his study of the material.

"Tate? I have to take a call. Will you be okay?" Rogan stood for a moment before she turned.

"I will. You need to do what you have to. That's not a problem." Her troubled eyes sought the kitchen doorway. "I'll go back and talk to Austin in a moment. I just need to try and understand what is happening. And I am not sure that I can."

"Austin will go over it with you." Rogan hugged her again and walked away, troubled that he had to but knowing that he had no choice.

Tate slid back into her chair, her eyes on Austin. He glanced at her, holding up a finger for her to wait to speak.

"Tate?" Austin sat back at long last, his eyes assessing her. He saw the distress that she was under and was disturbed at that. He knew that she had been open and honest with him.

"Austin? What did you find? I don't understand what is going on with all this." Her finger flicked the pile of paper in front of her.

"This is interesting material. I will need to research it, as you are aware. Tell me about your father."

Tate shrugged, her eyes thoughtful.

"I don't know what I can say. I don't even have a photo of him any more. Mom couldn't handle that and destroyed all the photos. I don't remember him at all, I was just so young, around four or so when he died. I am not sure that I can tell you much. Mom never talked about him."

"I see. This deepens what I need to look at. And I am working on it. We haven't been able to identify the shooter as yet. We are pulling videos from businesses in the area, searching for that person. We haven't been able to find any photos as yet, but we are speaking with the workers in the area, the street people, the people at the shelter." He grinned suddenly. "You are missed in the shelter and mission, Tate."

"I am? I thought they would be glad to have me gone from there."

"Not at all. You have endeared yourself to them. They are searching as well. First for Rogan's sake and then for yours. I am sure one of them will come back with information for us." Austin paused

---

as his phone chimed and excused himself to take a call. He stood, his eyes on Tate as she picked up the photo of her father and studied it. He sighed. Can't my friends find their ladies without danger? Guess not, Lord. Protect these two, please.

Chapter 10

Rogan walked slowly back through the house, his thoughts still on the conference call that he had just ended. The Board was wanting to bring in another worker, this time in the office, to help ease his burden, particularly now as he was a newlywed. He had had no condemnation from them. In fact, they had congratulated him and planned a meal in the next week where they and their spouses could meet with Rogan and Tate, just to welcome Tate to the family.

Tate worked away at the counter, preparing their meal as best she could. She was frustrated with the sling and finally removed it, grimacing with pain for a moment before she just turned back to her task. Her thoughts were on the papers, a frown flickering across her face every once in a while. *Why, Mom? Why hide Dad's information from me? I wanted to know him and you just refused. And just where are you anywhere? Lord, I can't do this. I need my Mom and she's not available. Who do I turn to?*

Rogan reached past Tate for their plates, startling her. He set the plates down and just gathered her close to him, feeling the wetness on his T-shirt as she wept. He sighed. He was no good with lady's tears or so he thought.

"Tate? What's wrong, my love?"

"It's just everything. I need my Mom and she's not here. I have no idea where she is. Who do I turn to?"

Rogan sighed himself. This was out of his league, he thought, even as he wrapped her tighter in his arms.

"Mom will talk with you, if you want. If not, Cara Fitzsimmons will."

Tate nodded

"That's Brownie's mom, right. They were at our wedding. I don't remember who all was."

"That's okay. Brownie is a good friend of mine. He and his wife went through stuff as did other friends of ours. Why don't we have some of them over later this week? You can meet them, hear their stories. And I know that they will work on it all to try and solve this for us." Rogan groaned as his phone kept chiming. He pulled it out, reading the text before he grinned in relief. "And I also have an acquaintance who finds people no one else can. We can contact her later and see what she can do for us."

"Okay." Tate moved backward, wiping at her face, not looking up at Rogan. His kiss on her forehead made her jump and then made her feel safe and cherished. "When?"

"How be we eat and then I'll call her? I don't think she'll mind." He frowned as the doorbell rang. "Were we expecting anyone?"

"I have no idea. Do you?" Tate stood and watched as Rogan walked away, hearing his surprised

---

tone of voice and then other voices. She watched as Rogan returned with a couple just older than them.

"Tate, this is Abe and Emma Finlay. Brownie said something to them and they are here to help. No, don't worry about stretching our meal. They brought enough for all of us." Rogan quickly reached to seat Tate, seeing her shaking for a moment.

Abe and Emma shared a look. God had prompted Emma to go to Abe that morning and simply state that they needed to find Rogan. He was in danger and needed Emma's help.

Conversation was general over the meal. Abe looked at Emma and then the couple sitting across from the.

"Can we spend some time in prayer, Rogan, Tate? Then Emma has information for you. And yes, she has sent it on to Austin."

Raising their heads, Tate shared a look with Rogan before she simply sat and stared at Emma. Just who was she, Tate wondered.

"Tate, I run a firm called Trackers. I started it years ago and have a number of people who work for me. I search for people and find them. Don't ask me how. I can't explain it. However, that being said, I do have information on your family. I understand that a private investigator has been around. He is legitimate. He approached me before he came to see you, asking if I could start the investigation. He is a friend of your father's from years ago. He has never been satisfied with what happened to him."

"He did? He is? I wondered. There seemed something familiar about him, but I just wasn't sure.

———

Can we contact him?" Tate shared a look with Rogan once more, hope on her face before it faded. "I don't really remember my father. Mom got rid of any pictures of him but wouldn't tell me why."

"That is part of what I've been investigating. A member of Abe's security team has a wife who researches family trees. She has looked into yours and has given me a copy for you and for the investigator as well."

"That's Austin. You know him from Brownie's problem."

"We do. I have spoken with him. Your town police chief was kind enough to die me that information." Abe and Emma shared a look. "It is concerning, Tate, that you were targeted and shot. I can't get a sense of why, and that is unusual for me. I am digging in deeper and deeper. I promise to keep you updated."

"Just tell me one thing. Was Dad involved in criminal activities?" Tate was desperate to hear that he wasn't.

"As far as I can determine, he was not." Emma gave a small smile at the deep breath that Tate released. "Nor is your mother. Go over what we have brought you and then call me. I mean that. Call me at any time, even if you just need to talk to someone. Abe and I had an adventure as we call it as have many friends. We don't understand exactly what you are going through, but we can share our stories with you and help you find some peace and comfort."

Chapter 11

The next day, Tate was determined to go through the paperwork. She sorted it and then began to read from the earliest date, rising at one point to fetch a pad of paper and a pen. Her notes covered many pages of the pad. Sitting back at last, Tate stretched and then rose, rubbing at her shoulder. She squinted at the clock and was dismayed. Rogan would be home shortly for supper. She had not started that very meal and hurried towards the kitchen, stopping as she realized that she really couldn't make a meal.

Rogan locked the door behind him, toeing off his shoes and moving them to the closet. He shifted the paper bag that he was carrying and approached the kitchen, finding Tate in tears as she stood at the open refrigerator door. Dropping the bag, he simply swept her into his arms, a kiss to her forehead, and a prayer uttered for her.

"Tate? What's wrong, my love?"

"It's suppertime, and I just can't make anything. I'm a failure as a wife." Tate choked on her tears.

"It's okay, my love. I sent a text but you mustn't have got it. I picked up something at the diner. Joey called me and told me to stop by. He sent our meal."

"He did? Why would he do that?"

"Because it's who he is. He considers anyone connected to the mission and the shelter as family. That now includes you."

"It does? That's a strange way to do things."

"It's how our town is, my love. They take care of their people. You're one of us now."

"Okay. So what did he send?" Tate reached for the bag and looked into it. "This smells delicious." She pulled out the containers. "Roast beef and the fixings. This is wonderful." A smile lit up her face, causing Rogan to stop in his tracks and stare at her, amazed at her beauty and that she was his.

Rogan sat back at last, his eyes on his phone as he pulled up a message. He frowned for a moment before he looked up at Tate. How did he tell her what Austin had said? That someone was looking for her and it wasn't for her good.

"Rogan? You're troubled. What is it?"

Rogan rose, clearing the table, and then making them fresh tea. He disappeared into the living room before returning and reaching for her hand.

"Come, let's sit in the other room, my love. We need to spend some time in prayer before we discuss what Austin has sent me. It's concerning and I am not sure how we can keep you safe."

"You're doing God's work, Rogan. It's in His hands. We can do all we can to protect both of us, but we can't move outside of His will."

Rogan nodded as he wrapped her in his arms, careful of her shoulder. He thought through what she said and realized that she was correct. But it still worried him. He didn't want to lose her and that was something that he needed to work through with his Heavenly Father.

"Rogan?" Tate's voice broke the silence after he had prayed. "What did Austin say? Has he any information of what we gave him?"

"No, he's still working through that. He has a number of cases that he is investigating and can't devote all his time to ours, although he would like to. He did say that there is word on the street that someone is looking for you. And it isn't for your good. Austin hasn't been able to confirm just why or who as yet."

"And he won't. Whoever it is will stay hidden as much as they can, now won't they?" Tate was lost in thought, Rogan just watching the conflicting emotions chasing each other across her face.

"You're deep in thought."

Tate turned to him.

"I am. I just don't know who would want that. I don't remember making any enemies. In fact, I have very few friends in whatever town I have lived in. So, I am at a loss."

"We know that, my love. That's what we're all trying to determine for you. Emma said she would have more material this week. She'll send it on. She is very concerned, I know that for sure. Abe has offered to come through and up our security for us."

"That would be good. I don't know how yours is." Tate went to rise and then settled back against him. "Rogan?"

"What, my love?"

Tate sat for a moment, her eyes on him, a puzzled look on her face.

"Rogan? You always call me your love. What's with that?"

"That's how I think of you, as my love. I didn't know that part of my heart was missing until you walked into it. I don't want to lose you, ever. We'll talk, my love, and decide where we want to go. For now, we need to worry about you."

"And you. They'll go after you to get to me, you know. I would suspect that they are following you all over the place."

Rogan began to laugh at the picture she had drawn.

"And you too. I hear my friends' ladies are plotting and planning to get together with you. If they do, they will have you out and about."

"And that is scary, Rogan. What if that man comes after me when I'm with them and they are hurt? How do I live with myself?" Tate rubbed at her arm, the incision beginning to throb.

"We'll deal with it. I can tell you that each of them had an adventure as well. You need to hear their stories." A grin creased his face.

Tate nodded, a sober look on her face.

"I guess. Rogan? I need to meet them. Can we have them here for a meal or is that too much?"

"Not too much for me, but I worry about you. You're not up to preparing a big meal."

"I know. What if we grill and then have salads and something for dessert?"

"That works. We'll do the meat and the others will bring the salads and desserts." His finger laid against her lips. "Don't protest. It's how we do things. We share meals like this. And we haven't done that in a while. We're due for that."

"Oh, okay."

Tate grew silent, content to be held. Rogan made sure that she was okay and then just sat as well, content to hold the love of his life in his arms. He wanted to tell her that but was afraid that he would drive her away. He had no idea what was in store for them but he knew Who was Iincharge and put all his faith and trust in his Heavenly Father.

Chapter 12

Rogan walked through the mission the next day, a grin on his face as he spoke with the men and women and yes, children who were there. They were important to him and he took the time to learn their names, dates of birth, and what they really wanted in life. He had been instrumental in finding work and homes and what have you for many of the ones who had passed through that very shelter.

A thought paused his steps, and he frowned before he spun and headed for his office.

"Austin? I had a thought. What if it wasn't Tate? What if Tate is being used to get to me?" Rogan was worried that he had brought trouble to his bride, trouble he had no idea what it was. His hand clenched at the phone headset, desperate to hear Austin say that it was Rogan all along and not Tate.

"Rogan? What was that? You think it's you?" Austin sat back in his chair, reaching for his pen and jotting down notes. "Why would you ask that?"

"Because we can find nothing with Tate to suggest she's a target. Me, on the other hand? Yeah, I could be just because of the nature of my work and the shelter and mission. I can't go into details about the residents past or present but my gut is saying this is what it is."

"Okay, so if it is you, how do we find the person?" Austin sat forward, pulling up his email

---

program and sending off a message to Emma. He was surprised at how quickly she responded that she had had that thought and had information that someone would drop off for him. "Emma's working that."

"She is? That doesn't surprise me." Rogan paced his office, a hand running through his hair, a troubled look on his face. "How do we do this, then?"

"Do what? Keep both of you safe? We can't lock you up, either one of you. So, just be cautious where you go. Keep an eye out for anyone around you. And it may be someone you know, not necessarily a stranger."

"You just had to say that, didn't you?" Rogan stared out the window, his eyes on a ramshackle car that had stopped in front of the mission before moving on. He frowned. He had seen it around before but never had it stop. Was this the car that the culprit was driving?

"I did. Now, stay safe, the both of you. I have to run but I'll be in touch this evening or tomorrow morning to discuss this further." Austin set his phone down. Rogan's question was troubling, and he just had to leave it for the moment. Other cases and interviews were demanding his attention.

Rogan turned to his desk, sitting behind it and staring at the paperwork that had accumulated. He had no choice. He had to work through it. There were applications for grants and whatnot that had to go in.

Raising his head, Rogan smiled and rose to his feet, heading for the hallway, to stand and stare at Tate. Tate stared back, a small smile on her face, deep in conversation with a young girl of around four years. Tate sat on the floor, letting the little one sit on her knee, her mother hovering close just in case she jarred Tate's shoulder.

The cook from the shelter stopped beside Rogan, her eyes moving between Tate and Rogan. She handed him a folder with invoices in it and then paused, a smile tracing on her face. Tate had been one of the few in the shelter who didn't seem to fit. *She's a lady,* the cook thought, an*d shouldn't have been here. I am glad that Rogan and Tate are married. They suit each other.*

"That little one won't let Tate leave, you know that, don't you?" The cook laughed as Rogan nodded.

"I know. That's okay with Tate, though. She loves the little ones." Rogan flipped through the folder. "These are all for now?"

"They are. We're okay for supplies for now." The cook hesitated. "What can we do for you and Tate, Rogan?"

Shrugged, Rogan stared at Tate, finding her attention on the little one cuddling up to her. He had a vision of Tate and his own little one doing that and that stopped him in his tracks. He had no idea if Tate would stay with him or not. That wasn't even on the table right now. Right now? It was enough that she was with him and that he would do his best to keep

---

her safe. He walked back to his office, turning to the invoices and losing track of time.

A sound startled him and he looked up, surprised to find Tate sitting across from him, her head tilted as she watched him. Her smile lit up her face as she saw his head raise.

"You were deep into that, Rogan."

"I was. Just invoices for supplies. Where's your young friend?" He grinned as her smile widened.

"She's off with her mom. Something about ice cream." She sighed. "She's so lucky, to have someone buy her ice cream. Mom didn't have the money for that when I was young."

Rogan stared at her, then gathered up the paperwork and locked it into a drawer. He rose, his hand out for hers.

"Come on. Ice cream sounds just wonderful. I am glad that you suggested it."

"I did?" Tate shook a finger at him. "How safe is that for us to do?"

Rogan stopped, his hand tightening on hers.

"We will continue to live, Tate. We are not running from him or her. We go about our daily walk. Which reminds me. Two days from now is Sunday."

"I know. This is going to be hard." She sounded disgruntled at the thought.

"It's okay. Most of the ones who go to the service you already know from here. The others?

They have been after me to get married, telling me that I need a helpmeet. Young ladies have been introduced to me."

"And why didn't you follow up on that?" Tate held her breath, not sure if she wanted to hear her answer.

"I was waiting for you, Tate. Just waiting for God to bring you into my life." His kiss hit her forehead even as she stared up at him, wonder in her eyes.

Chapter 13

A week later, Tate paced the house and then the outdoors. She was bored, she decided, not used to not having freedom to do what she wanted. She had no vehicle, even though she had a driver's license, but refused to ask Rogan to use his. Tate sighed, turning in a circle, trying to find the person who was watching her. It was a given that someone was. She had talked to Austin, and he had warned her that she could expect that. She had asked what all that she should be looking for and he had been honest with her. Tate had simply nodded, said it was about what she expected, and just how did she go about her life. Austin had given a grim smile and then walked away, knowing that their case was growing cold. There had been no new information that he could use. He couldn't investigate feelings and presumed sightings.

Tate finally walked around to the front of the house, finding Rori walking towards her. She frowned for a moment before she smiled. A person to talk to. That was what she needed. She was continuing with her proofreading but it really didn't fill that much of her day.

"Rori? Aren't you working today?" Tate reached to hug Rori. She had not been a hugger until she met Rori and Rori just moved in to hug her every time she saw her,

"No, I'm all done for the day. You need to get out and to the stores. I know that you do." Rori grinned at her sister-in-law.

"I do." Tate listened to the sounds of nature and the sounds of cars moving along the street, with the occasional closing of a door. "I do need to. Are you free to do just that?"

"I am. Come on. Let's grab what you need and lock up. I have a special store to show you today. It's run by a friend of mine and has such wonderful items."

Flushed with laughter, Tate finally stopped in front of a small shop.

"You need to stop, Rori. You're as bad as your brother for teasing."

Rori broke up into heavier laughter.

"He does love to tease, but it is never cruel. He says he finds humour helps with the people that he meets and cares for. I'll let you in on a secret. The more he teases, the more he thinks of you and loves you."

Tate blinked for a moment, not quite sure what Rori meant.

"It's like that, is it?" She turned in a circle. "Someone is watching us, Rori."

"I know. They have been all the time we've been wandering around here." She reached for the shop door, pulling it open. "This is the shop. Wendy has such gorgeous trinkets and gifts. I know that you will like her stock. At least, I hope you do."

Austin had been watching from across the street, not quite believing that Tate was wandering around in the open like she was. But then again, she could not stay locked away. That would not be good for her and it certainly would not bring out whoever it was that was stalking her. And stalking her was what they had determined was happening. Just why? That was a question they were still working through.

A hand held up to the traffic, Austin ran across the street, his eyes on a youth who appeared to be very interested in the shop. Not that it was a shop that he would be found in. His grubby appearance belied that very thought. The youth spun as he heard Austin's running footsteps and then took off running. Austin slid to a stop and shook his head. He knew the youth, knew his connections in the town, and knew that he was deeply involved in crime. Only they had never been able to catch him to prove anything.

Rori looked around as she heard footsteps, relaxing as Austin approached them. Tate looked around as well, frowning at Austin.

"Austin? What did I do now that I shouldn't have?"

Austin gave a grim smile.

"Nothing, Tate. Absolutely nothing. We can't keep you locked away. That's a given. But someone was watching through the window. He has likely been following you."

"There was? I know that I'm being followed and watched. We've seen evidence in the early morning dew and found footprints in the front garden. Why didn't we call you?" She stared at Austin as his

---

mouth opened and then snapped closed. "Because we can't prove anything. That's why."

Tate moved away, looking for something, only she wasn't sure what. Her fingers traced the delicate ornaments and then reached for a sun catcher. The rainbow design was just what she needed. She needed to be reminded daily that God's promises were true. That He had promised to protect her and guide her. Only sometimes, she didn't feel His presence. She and Rogan had talked about that. Rogan had admitted that sometimes he felt the same way.

Rori watched her walk away before she spoke.

"What do we do, Austin? How do we do this? Neither one will want to be locked up totally. Rogan can't and Tate won't."

"I know, Rori. I know. It's difficult to be a family member and watch this." Austin grew silent, thinking of the past and a memory that he had buried. His aunt had been stalked and it took months and a lot of danger to capture the stalker. That was part of why he became a police officer

Tate turned at that moment, catching Austin's attention. He frowned, trying to determine just who she reminded him of. And remind him of someone she did.

———

Chapter 14

Pacing through the house, Rogan was on a search. He stopped for a moment, his eyes on the letter that he held in a shaking hand. It contained only a photo of Tate and Rori, catching them standing in front of a shop. He drew in a deep breath. This was just adding to the stress that he was under, knowing that both of the ladies in his life were being threatened. He could not understand why. Austin has been silent when he had called him, demanding something be done.

"Rogan? I'll be by later on my way home. Stay in the house if you can. This is getting worse, you know."

"I know. I don't like it." Rogan had tossed his phone onto the kitchen table and turned. Tate had to be here somewhere.

Tate rose from where she had been kneeling, working in one of the gardens, watching with a frown as Rogan walked toward her and simply swept her close to his heart. They stood before Rogan stared down at the garden.

"Working your magic?"

"Trying to. Your gardens are in good shape." Tate turned in Rogan's arms, looking around the yard.

"Rori has been working on them as she can. But with her work, she is limited to what she can do."

"That's what she said. Rogan? Any news?" Tate was desperate to know that it was all over and they could get on with their lives. Only she was afraid that Rogan would tell her to leave. She stood, the sounds and songs of nature ringing in her ears. She loved that, being outside, grubbing in the dirt, watching God's creation grow and flourish. Tate felt closer to God when she was outside.

Rogan just held her closer.

"Not really. Austin said he's stopping by on his way home. I have no idea what he has discovered. He has never said."

"Okay." Tate sighed, a deep deep sigh, weary of what she was facing but not weary of being held by Rogan. He made her feel loved, cherished, treasured, safe. And that was in just such a short period of time.

Rogan stood for a moment before he reached for Tate's hand. Someone was around, he could feel them. And that worried him. He turned them to the house, rushing that way, but didn't make it in time. The men who appeared in front of them stopped them in their tracks. Rogan's hand tightened on Tate's, not quite sure what was happening. Tate gave a light whimper, recognizing the man.

"Tate? We've been looking for you. You need to come with us."

Tate started to back up, shaking her head.

"No. No, I don't. I don't know you. Rogan?"

"You're not going anywhere, my love. These men will not take you anywhere." Rogan had spied Austin approaching, David with him.

"But we are." The man reached for Tate's arm, finding Rogan stepping between them. His fist was out, striking Rogan in the jaw, causing him to stumble backward and tumble to the ground. Tate tumbled with him, a scream torn from her. The man's hand was on her wrist, tugging her to her feet, as Austin ran forward.

Austin's hands were out and the man was quickly handcuffed. David had handled the man's partner, quickly cuffing him as well. Austin shoved his prisoner towards David who was on his radio asking for assistance. Turning to Rogan, he found him already on his feet, a hand rubbing at his jaw and his other arm tight around Tate.

"Austin? How did you and David manage to get here just at the right time?"

Austin gave a grim smile.

"Your neighbour across the street? He's been watching their car drive around all day and then parking in front of your place. It didn't belong so he called it in. I was already on my way. David was on duty and caught the call. What happened?"

Tate grew angry in her fear and terror. She shook for a moment, finding Rogan's arm tightening around her.

"What happened? We're out here. In our yard. Minding our own business on our own property. And they appeared. They wanted me to go with them. No, demanded that. Rogan? Your face? He hit you."

"I know, my love. I know. I'm okay. I was moving backward as he swung at me. That put me off balance. That's why I fell." He stared across the yard for a moment, at a loss for words, not as he usually was.

"Rogan?"   Austin watched as David and another officer shoved the men around the house, the wooden gate swinging shut behind them. "I would put a lock on that if I were you. Just to have some security. Now, let's get Tate sitting down before she falls down." He pointed at their back patio.

Tate simply shook her head and walked away, heading into the house. She had prepared a salad supper and cold meats as it had been a warmer day. Loading the food, plates and utensils on a tray, she turned, finding Rogan beside her and Austin as well. Rogan took that tray from her as Austin loved another tray with their mugs and the coffee, cream, and sugar.

Siting back after the meal, Austin studied the yard, finding the peace for which he had been searching all day. He listened to the sounds of the twilight as the day critters crept to their rest and the night critters came out. He tilted his head, hearing the sound of the pond from behind the yard.

Rogan watched him and then turned his attention to Tate, finding her sitting with her eyes closed, a peaceful expression on her face. He smiled. *Yes,* Rogan thought. *It is peaceful here. We all need this.*

Chapter 15

"Austin? You were heading here for a reason?" Tate turned to him, her eyes thoughtful. Lord, let him tell us that this is over. I don't know how much more we can take.

"I was." Austin gave a grin and then sobered. "I just wanted to see how you two were. Whether you had come up with anything else to tell me. I didn't expect to walk into an attempted abduction. What happened?"

Tate stared at him, her mouth dropping open for a moment. Rogan gave a grin, reaching for her hand and squeezing it in sympathy with her feelings.

"We were walking back towards the house and they were just there." Tate was upset, that was obvious. "Where did they come from?"

"They have been in the neighbourhood all day. Your neighbour finally called in a strange car that kept circling the block." Austin pulled out his notebook. "What did they say to you?"

"Just that they had been looking for me and I was to go with them." Tate was puzzled, a frown appearing on her face. "I don't know them. I don't know that I had ever seen them before. At least, I don't think I have."

Rogan nodded in agreement.

"I don't know them at all. I can ask around the mission if I can have a photo."

"No, Rogan. Let us do that." Austin was frustrated. This was not going as he had expected. "So, tell me, how are you both really doing?"

Rogan shrugged, his eyes on Austin, feeling Tate's hand tighten on his.

"I guess we're okay. It's fatiguing, Austin, to be on guard all the time. I worry about Tate when I'm away. And I know that she's the same. She worries about me when I'm away. But I can't take her to the mission with me. Not at present. We've agreed that would put the residents at great risk."

"That it would." Austin rubbed at his neck as he thought through what could be done, finally shaking his head. "I don't know what to suggest. We've talked many times."

"That we have." Rogan turned to Tate, finding her sitting with her eyes closed. "Can we spend some time in prayer? We need that."

"That we do. And remember that you both were prayed for in the Garden all those years ago." Austin caught a movement from Tate, finding her nodding. "Tate?"

"We were. I keep reminding myself of that. It's hard to remember sometimes but I do try. Rogan, that would make a good message for you to bring."

Rogan grinned at her even as he reached to hug her.

"That I can. Austin, what else can you tell us?"

"There's not a lot we can. No shooter has been identified. We have searched and asked and come up empty. That tells me that it was a professional."

"Professional?" Tate's voice rose as she spoke. "Professional? Sure. That would make sense. What happened with that young man from today?"

"The one who was watching you? He has been released. There was nothing to charge him with, but his photo is out there with the patrols. They will be watching him."

"I see. So he could be following us and we would not know that. I don't like it but there's not much we can do, is there?"

"He could be. We can't stop him. That being said, we have offers who are offering to play bodyguard for you both. The chief has agreed and is drawing up a schedule. He'll be speaking with you both as to what your days are like."

"They can't do that!" Tate was dismayed and then was on her feet, running for the house, the door closing behind her.

Rogan stood, his eyes on the door, wanting to go to Tate but knowing that he had to let her have this time. She needed it. He would track her down in a bit.

Austin had risen as well, his eyes shifting between the two. He sighed. This was not how it was to have happened, he decided.

"Look, Rogan. I'm off. Let me help you clean up and then I'll be on my way."

"Thanks, Austin. It's okay. You can get on your way. There are not a lot of dishes. I can handle that."

Austin nodded, opened his mouth to speak, and then walked away, his heart and mind troubled. It would only get worse for them, he knew, and that frightened him. He hated to see his friends going through this. He nodded to himself. Brownie and Keegan would be the ones that he should send their way. Austin had no way of knowing that Brownie and Keegan had already been in touch with the couple and were planning on having a meal with them in the next couple of days.

Chapter 16

Two weeks later, Rogan stood in the parking lot of the mission, watching as police officers swarmed around the cars. A bomb threat had come in, but they didn't know if it was related to himself or to Tate. Hearing running footsteps, he turned but didn't make it all the way around before a body hit him. Tate had found him and he could feel the terror and desperation in the way she clung to him.

"Rogan? You're okay? I was so afraid when I heard."

"You were? How did you get here?" Rogan looked around for whoever it was that

"David. He was not on duty but he came and found me. Austin called, to let me know that you were okay. He was around, he said, but was called to another scene." Tate blinked, trying to clear her eyes of tears, not realizing that her face with streaked with them.

Rogan simply tightened his hold, his chin resting on the top of her head. He was furious, he decided. He didn't know who had left the bomb but it had threatened people and the mission. He would need to work through that anger, he knew, but right now? All he cared about was making sure his people were safe, and the most important one he held in his arms.

———

76

David approached him, his eyes steady on the couple. He had been running errands when Austin had called, asking that he find Tate and then Rogan. Austin had explained what was happening. David had not hesitated at all, knowing that Tate would be beside herself with worry. She had just stared at him, swung the door closed and locked it and almost ran to his car, desperate to find her groom. David had shaken his head and then shut the car door after her, running around to slide behind the wheel.

"What do you know, David?" Tate's head was in constant movement, searching for what or who she just didn't know.

"Not a lot. There was a bomb threat at the mission. Rogan is safe as are the people there."

"Oh, thank God. I was so worried about them."

David pulled to a halt down the street from the mission, behind the emergency vehicles. A hand on Tate's arm kept her in her seat.

"Let me get out first, Tate." David's voice was firm. "We want to put officers around you as we walk you to Rogan. This would be a very good time to grab you and disappear with you. In the confusion, no one would really notice. Their attention is on the parking lot."

"I know. I just want to find him. Please, David?"

Walking toward the parking lot, Tate's full focus was on finding Rogan. David knew that and shared a look with the officers surrounding them. He sighed to himself. This was not to have happened, he thought. They don't need this, now do they, Lord? I want this solved and now but that won't happen. We don't have enough information to even keep the investigation going. And that I fear is exactly what will happen - that we will have to let it go to a cold case.

Rogan looked up at last to find David standing beside them, his eyes on the crowd. Officers surrounding them, backs to the couple, watching the gathering crowd. Despite the best efforts of the authorities, word had gotten out and spectators were gathering. The news media were there, speculation rampant among the reporters. Rogan knew that they would soon track him down and he just didn't want to talk to them. It was too personal, he decided. He felt a hand on his shoulder and looked around. Cameron Fitzsimmons stood there. Cameron was a fellow pastor but more importantly a friend. Brownie's father knew Rogan well, and knew that he would not be party to planning anything, even though that was how one of the news reporters was trying to play it

"Cameron?" Rogan's voice held the question that he would not ask.

"Rogan. I'm here for support. You know that. The board chair called me. They have uttermost faith in you. I was asked to relay that to you. I was also asked to make sure that you and Tate are safe. If that means I take over here for now, that's a decision you and I will come to."

"I know, Cameron. It may come to that. Where's Brownie?" Rogan looked around for his friend, Tate simply standing listening to their words.

—

"He's on duty but is off soon. He said he and Keegan would head for your home."

"Thank you. We'll head that way soon, but right now, I need to stay. Tate? Do you want to go back home with Cameron?" Rogan waited patiently, knowing that Tate had heard him but was in the process of trying to understand what was happening.

Tate looked up at him at long last, a puzled look in her eyes.

"No, I think that I want to wait with you. Will you be long?"

"I have no idea. I have given my statement and can leave but Austin asks that I stay for a bit."

"Okay. I want to stay with you." She looked around. "Is that man here?"

"More than likely." Rogan shared a look with Cameron, who simply nodded.

"Cara is heading over to your place as well, Rogan. Where are your parents and Rori?"

"Rori is likely at work. No, that's not true. She had a conference out of town and she's due back tomorrow. Mom and Dad? They're on holiday. They didn't want to leave but I asked them to. They can't put their lives on hold just because I'm going through something."

"But they will, Rogan. You know that they will." Cameron pulled out his phone that kept chiming. "Brownie's at your place. It looks as if someone broke into it."

Tate spun to stare at him.

———

"I locked up." Tate was horrified. "If I had been home?"

Rogan hugged her tighter, his eyes on Austin who had approached and stopped as he heard Cameron's words.

"We know that you did. You always do. And you likely would have disappeared." Rogan's eyes slid closed, the very picture of that in his mind. "And I don't want to lose you"

Chapter 17

Later that afternoon, Tate stood in her kitchen, arms wrapped around herself. She could hear conversation around her and then the sound of a vacuum. Rogan's friends were helping to clean up the mess left by the break-in and then the crime scene techs as they moved through. She was puzzled. There was nothing taken. That concerned Rogan, who had just wrapped her into his arms once more, both needing the contact with one another.

Cara, Brownie's mother, approached, an arm coming around the younger woman. She frowned as Tate jumped and then relaxed.

"Tate? What can we do for you?"

Tate shrugged, not sure of anything any more.

"I really don't know. I want this over, but it doesn't seem to be. I worry about Rogan. Who does this?"

Keegan had approached, her hands reaching for the coffee and tea pots, setting them on a tray already loaded with mugs, spoons, cream, sugar. She shared a look with Cara before she spoke.

"This is what they want, Tate. They want you afraid, uncertain, ready to run, ready to hide, watching everyone around you who are friends or strangers. Not talking with anyone in case you bring danger to them."

Tate had turned as Keegan had begun to speak. She hadn't heard the men stopping in the doorway or seen Brownie reach for the tray and move back into the living room. Rogan breathed a sigh of relief and a prayer of thanks. God was using Keegan to reach through to Tate, he could see. That was what being a community of faith is, he thought. Friends who can understand to some extent and reach through where someone else might not be able to.

"Is that what happened to you?" Tate's voice was barely a whisper and they had to struggle to hear her.

"It is. Every victim of crime goes through the same thing. They doubt themselves, doubt those around them, don't sleep, don't eat. That's what we faced. Friends of ours did as well. It's what happens. And it is no reflection on you. No reflection on where your faith is. God is here, Tate, right here. He walks beside you every single step. He has already gone before you in this. God knew before time began what you would face and who it is that is long this. He understands. Don't forget that Jesus prayed for you in the garden."

Tate blinked rapidly, her mind trying to absorb what Keegan was saying. She turned in a frantic motion, searching for Rogan, finding him reaching for her, to cradle her close. This seemed to be a favourite and familiar position, she thought, but she welcomed his touch. He made her feel safe and secure.

The group finally found seats in the living room, finding seats. Austin dropped his briefcase beside his chair, his eyes on Cameron before they all bowed and brought the young couple to the throne of God. *They were no further ahead really,* Austin mused. *And that frightens me. Not much does any more, but this does. I don't want to see them go through what the others have. And there have been many. But God did provide protection and relief and closure for all of them.* Austin raised his head, his eyes on Brownie, who was watching Rogan and Tate intently. He nodded before he heard Rogan speaking.

"Austin? What can you tell us?"

"Not a lot at the moment, Rogan. I'm not the one investigating the bomb today. That is someone else but she will be in touch with you in the next day or so. I won't speculate on that at all. We just need to concentrate on what we have going on ourselves."

"It's related, do you think?" Brownie spoke up. He had been talking with the patrol officers who had been on the scene and that was the general feeling.

"It may be. I don't have the details to confirm or deny that, Brownie." Austin stared at his notes, not sure what he could say. "Tate? Your mother? We're tracking her steps. She is still alive from what we can determine and seems to have been following you from town to town."

"She has? But she hasn't contacted me. Not at all." Tate's lips trembled as she fought back her emotions. "I want to find her and ask her why she did what she did. What did I ever do to her to cause this?"

"You did nothing, not that we can find out. The authorities in the last town that you lived in? They know where she has been living and are working

---

towards contacting her. She is hiding, Tate, and we want to know why and how it relates to what you are going through." Austin paused, needing to ask a difficult question. "Have you felt that you have been followed and watched?"

Tate stared at him, her mind puzzling through his question.

"No, not that I have known or felt. I just moved from town to town because I was restless and didn't find one that I felt at home in. Until this town. As you know, I was planning on moving into an apartment. Only he backed out of the deal. Do you know why?"

"We do, Tate. We have spoken with him. Someone told him that you were into drugs and crime. He took their word as they were from this town and you weren't."

"That bizarre. And disturbing. Who would do that?" Tate was troubled, tears pooling in her eyes, as she stared past Austin towards the framed photos on the wall. A puzzled look grew on her face and then she was on her feet, moving towards the photos and taking one down. "This was not here this morning. I don't know these people or where they are. Who put it here?"

Rogan was on his feet, his hand out for the photo. It puzzled him too. He didn't know the people.

"Austin?" He turned as Austin reached for the photo.

"I think this is why they broke in. I'll take this and see what I can do with it." Austin walked away, his phone out to speak with his supervisor.

"And that's that, then." Tate turned, her eyes on each one gathered. "Can we pray? We need God's protection now more than ever."

Chapter 18

A week later, Rogan stood once more in the parking lot at the mission. It was a Saturday and warm. There were many people milling around for the monthly lunch that the mission provided. It was always well attended by the residents of the shelter, the people who chose to live on the streets for some reason and those supporters of the mission and shelter who were able to be there. He could hear Tate and Rori as they laughed with some small children. Rogan turned, a smile on his face as he watched Tate hold a young girl of around two, receiving many hugs from that little girl.

Brownie and Austin stopped beside him. They were scanning the crowd, knowing that this was one avenue of disappearance that was available to their stalkers.

"Rogan? Anything new?"

Rogan shook his head, not moving his gaze from Tate. How he loved that lady, he thought. And she was opening up to him, her love for him evident. She had told him that very morning that she loved him and that she had never expected to find anyone to love her. She had always felt unlovable. He has simply hugged her tight, kissed her, and then prayed for both Tate and for their marriage.

"No. Austin? Any word on that photo?"

"Not really. The techs are working through it as am I. We haven't been able to identify them as yet." Austin looked around as he heard footsteps. "Tate?"

"I know. You don't know who or why. Of course, you won't. They're hiding and in plain sight." Tate looked around, her arms wrapping around herself. "They can be out here anywhere and we wouldn't know that."

"That is true. That is why there are a number of officers around here in plain clothes. It's what we do. They support you and Rogan and they support the work that is done here. It makes their life easier with the support that the mission and church provide. We have one of the lower crime rates in this area than most towns do."

"That's true, Tate." Rogan wrapped an arm around her. "It is how our town works." He groaned as his phone chimed. This was not the time for something like this. He reluctantly pulled it out and paused as he read the message. "Emma's in touch, Austin. She's sending material to you."

"Emma is? Then, she'll have found something." Austin didn't say that he had reached out to her, providing a copy of the photo to her and asking for her help.

"She will have or Jace will." Brownie grinned suddenly. "Think her husband will show up with his security team?"

Rogan began to laugh, drawing a frown from Tate.

"It's okay, Tate. Abe, Emma's husband, has a security team that he has offered in the past to provide security for those of us in danger. We'll talk through anything like that. Unless it's a matter of life and death."

"I see. That's fine." Tate was distracted, following a woman who was walking around the edge of the crowd. "Mom? Mom's here?"

Austin stared at her and then followed her line of sight. He was away, Brownie with him, heading for the woman and following her. Austin finally reached her and stopped her, his identification out to prove who he was. The woman paled and then nodded, walking away with the two men.

Keegan watched for a moment before she turned to Tate.

"Austin and Brownie will talk with her and determine if that is in fact her and why she is here in this town."

Rogan had had to step away to answer some questions from a board member but he stood where he could watch Tate. She was fading, he could tell, and he needed to get her home. Only, he couldn't leave. The board member was watching Rogan and then Tate.

"Take her home, Rogan. Take your bride home. And stay there."

Rogan stared at him, in shock.

"Go. Take Tate home. We'll manage for today. She needs you." The board member laid a hand on Rogan's shoulder and prayed for him.

"We'll take it week by week, Rogan. When you are on site, we will have security here. We have made those arrangements for you. You are a valued and treasured part of our mission family. We understand that it is difficult for you at this time. We get that. But you need to take care of your bride."

"I don't know what to say, Alan. Except thank you. I can do some work from home."

"That works. We trust you. And we understand that as a newlywed, you need to spend time with Tate, time that is not going to happen because of what you two are going through."

"Thank you, Alan. You board members are always great. You personify the hands and feet of God in what you do."

"That's our mission, Rogan. I am friends with Bruce and Barnabas Carey of The Barnabas Foundation. They are all supporters of us. This is their premise - to be encouragers to those around them. And they do it. We can do no less."

Rogan nodded, watching as Alan walked away, turning as he heard a voice beside him.

"Tag? You're here? Where's Ayron?"

"With your wife and Keegan. Sorry that we haven't been around. We've had to be out of town for a few weeks for business."

"Yes, you were. Listen, I'm heading home. Alan had told me to go. Are you two free?"

"We are. We want in on your adventure. I understand Brownie is tied up right now but Keegan has made plans with Tate to provide a meal for us. Did you know that?" Shay grinned at Rogan.

"That sounds like a plan. Let's head out." Rogan walked towards Tate, a hand reaching for hers.

Chapter 19

Tate stared at the document that she had just taken from an envelope. A summons? But what for? She began to shake in fear. Dropping the document on the kitchen table, she backed away, her hand covering her mouth to cover her mouth. Who would do this, she questioned? And why? She needed Rogan, only he wasn't there.

Keegan tapped at the back door, not having been able to get an answer at the front door. With the ease of friendship, she opened the door, peeking in and then stepping into the mudroom. Heading for the kitchen, she stopped abruptly, her eyes on Tate.

Tate had turned at the slight sound, her eyes huge with her fright. All she could think was that whoever it was had found her. She opened her mouth to scream and then snapped it shut as she recognized Keegan.

Keegan approached cautiously, her phone out to call Brownie. She knew that Tag and Ayron were heading that way shortly, but this was something that obviously could not wait.

"Tate?" Keegan's hand was out to grasp the badly shaking hand that Tate held out. "What happened?"

Tate was unable to stop herself from shaking.

"That!" She pointed at the table. "That! A summons of some kind. I don't know what it is."

Keegan approached the table, a finger out to turn over the paper. Tate was right. It was a summons. Only she had no idea why or what.

"Did you open it?" Keegan turned her head as Tate made a low sound. "Tate?"

"I didn't. I couldn't. Make it go away." Tate turned, stumbling as she moved, to drop into a corner of the kitchen, her knees drawn up and her arms wrapped around her head.

Rogan hit the door on the run, his car door slamming behind him. Keegan had reached him, simply stating that Tate needed him and that she was terrified. He frantically looked for her, following Keegan's finger as she pointed towards Tate. Rogan was on the floor, wrapping Tate in his arms, his head on hers.

"Sweetheart? My love? What happened?" Rogan was beginning to panic himself, not able to rouse Tate from the terror that gripped her. He looked up as Keegan stood near him. "Keegan?"

"She received a summons of some kind, Rogan. She hasn't looked at it. I didn't either, just to turn it over and see what it was."

"A summons?" Rogan reached to take the paper that Keegan was thrusting at him, a frown on his face before his eyes turned back to Tate.

"Yes. A summons. This is bizarre, Rogan." Keegan turned as she heard the doorbell and walked that way, peeking out to find Brownie and Austin there, with Tag and Ayron walking towards them.

Rogan studied the paper and then just dropped it to the floor. He would look at it later. Right now, though? Right now, Tate needed him. He shifted on the wood floor and raised her to his lap, his arms tightening around her as she began to sob. *This was so heart breaking,* he thought. *Lord? Where are You? My lady needs comfort and I don't think I can do that. Not today. This needs Your touch.*

Austin stood for a moment, assessing the situation, before he stooped and picked up the paper. A frown covered his face. He nodded as Brownie murmured that he would search outside, not expecting that he would find anything.

"Rogan? What is this?" Austin spoke quietly, not disturbing Tate as he did so.

"A summons of some kind. I haven't looked at it. Keegan said Tate hadn't either." Rogan shifted his clasp around his bride, his gaze shifting between Tate and their friends.

Austin studied his friends, his heart breaking for the couple. He couldn't see Tate's face as she had it hidden against Rogan. His eyes dropped to the summons and he frowned. This was not a legitimate one, he thought. He read through it, troubling thoughts raising in his mind. Brownie paused beside him, not saying anything.

"There's nothing outside?" Austin's voice was low.

"Nothing. That either came through the mail or was hand delivered. Rogan doesn't have video surveillance. We need to change that."

"I have cameras with me, Brownie." Tag spoke up. "I'll install them today. That's one of the reasons we're here today." He too watched Rogan and Tate. "Rogan?"

Rogan looked up, surprised to see how many people were there.

"Tag? You're here. That's right. You were to be here. Go ahead with the cameras. I'll set up the computer in a bit for you. And our phones."

"Take your time, Rogan. We'll get there." Tag walked away, Ayron moving to stand with Keegan.

"Keegan? How long?" Ayron turned to watch the activity or lack of it in the kitchen.

"An hour at least. I've been here for that long but I don't know how long it was since she found it."

"This is so bizarre." Ayron reached for the kettle, intent on making a cup of tea for Tate. "Austin will look into it."

Austin turned away, reading through the summons once more. He was more disturbed than before. The document purported to be a summons but it made no sense. It didn't say why it was issued, when she had to appear, or where.

Rogan spoke from beside him.

"It's not legitimate, is it? They figured that she'd see it and run. Then they would have grabbed her and disappeared with her."

"That was more than likely. With her freezing as she did in fear, that never happened. And with Keegan appearing? That also kept her safe in the house." Austin bit at his lip, knowing that he had to speak with Tate but she was still not responding. "How is she?"

"Petrified is how I would put it. She's not responding to me and that is unusual." Rogan sighed. "We need to call the paramedics. I may have to take her to the hospital, and I'm not comfortable doing that."

Rori stood in the doorway to the mudroom, having felt compelled to come. One look at Tate and she was on her knees, beginning her assessment. Tate didn't respond and that concerned her. Rogan moved to crouch down beside them, just watching. And praying. And pleading for it to be all over.

Chapter 20

An hour later, Tate huddled down in a corner of the couch, a blanket wrapped around her, a mug of tea clutched in her hands. She had refused to speak, even though Austin had tried his best. She had simply shaken her head, her eyes pleading with him to let her alone, at least for now.

Rogan stood with Brownie and Tag, deep in conversation in the kitchen. Keegan and Rori moved around the kitchen as well, making a simple meal for the group. Austin had finally left, taking the documentation with him. He needed to investigate it, but he had been called to another crime scene and that investigation took precedence at present.

"Tag? What do you suggest?" Rogan was desperate, feeling out of his league right then.

"I have installed the cameras where they will do the best work. You will receive alerts on your phones and computer. That way, if you're not home, you can call for police to attend." Tag was a retired officer and knew the danger his friends faced. He and Ayron had also been through danger as a couple as had a number of their friends.

"I see. Okay. But what else? Austin and Brownie had given advice, but they still seem to be getting to us."

"They will. They are watching you very closely. I saw evidence of that earlier today."

—

Brownie was worried more than he had been. The tracks that he had found had been tight to the house, in the gardens and then moving all through the yard. It was only a matter of time until they found their way into the house. And if that happened, Tate and likely Rogan would disappear. So far, they had not been able to. "We need to set up a really tight security system for you, Rogan. The cameras will help but we need to wire the doors and windows with sensors."

"I know. I don't know who to get." Rogan sighed, slumping down into a wooden chair at the table, not seeing the colourful tablecloth that Tate had found earlier that week. The colours matched the colours in the kitchen and contrasted with the white appliances.

"I have a friend or two. Joseph or Branigan will help." Tag moved away, intent on making that call. His eyes landed on Tate and saw that she was gradually coming around. "Rogan? Tate is more alert."

Rogan nodded, his feet tangling with one another as he rose, fatigue hitting in large waves. He had not been sleeping, staying awake to guard the love of his life, keeping Tate tight in his arms as she slept. He slipped down beside her, his arms tight around her. This is becoming a family position, he decided, holding Tate and begging God to end this and keep her safe. His own life he really didn't care about.

Keegan leaned against Brownie as she watched, her prayers rising as well. She was trying her best to come up with something that would help, but couldn't. She knew that friends were investigating as well, only there seemed to be a huge wall that seemed insurmountable.

"Brownie? What are we missing? We have to be missing something."

"I know, love. I know. There is something. Austin said that they found her mother but she's not talking and is refusing to even acknowledge Tate is her daughter. He did say that her mother had been following her from town to town." Brownie pulled his lip over his upper teeth. There had to be something that they were missing. Only, he had no idea what that was.

Rogan tilted his head to watch his bride's face, seeing the awareness of her surroundings that was returning. He sighed. This is not how the day was to have gone. He had been deep into his message for Sunday when Keegan had called.

Tate roused, surprised to see people in her home, people that she didn't know had arrived. She struggled for a moment before she heard Rogan's soft words of comfort and his prayer.

"Rogan? What happened? Why are they all here?" Tate was very confused sounding.

"Keegan walked in after you found a summons. Then she called in reinforcements. Austin has taken that paperwork."

"Summons? For what? I don't remember that." Tate's head went down on his shoulder. "Do I need to remember it?"

"You likely will. Austin will be back around," he said, wanting to talk with you. What all happened this morning?"

"I really don't know. I remember you leaving and then working around in the kitchen, just cleaning the house. I don't remember past that." Tate's troubled gaze studied the two couples who had taken seats in the living room. "Why don't I?"

"Shock can do that. Your mind will cover things to protect yourself." Brownie spoke up, having seen it on the job. "You may remember. You may not remember."

"I see. Okay. Was Rori here?"

"She was. She dropped in between her cases and assessed you. We were ready to take you to the hospital, you were that out of it." Keegan spoke up. "I saw you right after, Tate. You had no idea that I was here. I mean, you spoke to me for a bit and then just huddled down in a corner."

"I did? I don't remember. And I should." Tate stared at the ceiling, a troubled look on her face. "Where is God again in all this? I know He's here but I don't feel His presence. Not like I think I should."

"He's here, Tate." Tag spoke up. "I worked undercover for many years, from when I was a teenager. I saw and heard things no one should ever hear. But He was always with me. I know that He protected me over those years. He also protected Ayron and me when we had our troubles. There are times when we don't feel Him around us, but He is. He has promised never to leave us or forsake us. That is a promise that He will never break. Our feelings and humanness get in the way of this promise."

"Tag's right, love." Rogan picked up Tag's words. "God is here, with us, every step of the way. Let's spend some time in prayer, please, friends? Then we need to make some decisions, decisions that will be hard to make."

Chapter 21

Tate snuggled down tighter to Rogan, not feeling safe at all. She couldn't remember seeing that piece of paper but she felt the terror once more. Just why that was? She couldn't verbalize what her feelings were. Rogan's arms made her feel protected but somehow, she felt that he was threatened, just because he had stepped in and saved her from whatever it was. Her gaze moved around the room, taking in the soft yellow of the walls, the dark wood flooring, the comfortable furniture and knick-knacks. Tate's gaze stopped on the fireplace and she frowned. There was something off about it, but she wasn't sure what. Would someone have tampered with the gas?

"Rogan? Is the fireplace safe? I don't feel that it is."

The men's actions froze for a moment as they stared first at Tate and then at the fireplace. Tag was on his feet, heading for it, knowing that Tate may well have picked up on something. He frowned as the faint smell of gas hit his nose.

"People, we need to vacate and call in a gas man. I can smell gas and I shouldn't. Don't touch anything else."

Rogan watched as the gas technician entered his home and sighed. This is just getting better and better. I'm sorry, Lord. I'm just so tired of this, wanting it over and it just doesn't seem to be. I fear for my beloved bride, for our friends, for anyone who gets in the way. And not knowing who it is or why? That makes it just so much worse.

Daniel approached the group, the sun glinting off his badge. He had picked up the call when Brownie called it in, not quite sure what was going on.

"Brownie?" Daniel's quiet voice caught Brownie's ear and he turned before walking toward him. "I heard the call."

"Tate asked if someone tampered with the fireplace. I have no idea why. She seems to be thinking through how someone could get to her and hurt either her or Rogan."

"And she's correct. That's what we're hearing on the streets. That someone is looking for someone to do just that. But the fireplace? How did she do that?"

"I don't know. The tech is inside right now, to determine if in fact that it has been." Brownie watched as the tech exited the house and moved towards his truck, retrieving tools and what he needed. "And it looks as if it was. He turned off the gas before he went in."

Daniel paled, his hands clenching at his bullet-proof vest.

"And if they hadn't known, they would have turned on the fireplace and that would have been it." Daniel's thoughts ran wild for a moment. "Austin is aware and will head this way when he can."

"Thanks, Daniel. This is hard for them. I don't think that we have been terrorized like this before."

"No, I don't think that we have. In the bigger cities, yes, but not here in our small town. This is scary."

"It is." Tag had approached and listened to their conversation. "We need to find somewhere to hide them."

"And they won't go. I know Rogan. He will not leave his people. And Tate has been adamant that she will not run. She simply stated one day that she had been on the move for too many years and that she had found her safe haven here with Rogan." Brownie reached to hug Keegan, his eyes on Rogan and Tate as they just stood and spoke with the tech, who was showing them something.

Daniel walked toward them, catching the eye of the tech. The tech watched as Daniel stopped and then handed him some debris.

"She was right. This was tampered with. Not enough that a spark from something would have set it off, but enough that if they had lit the fireplace, there would have been an explosion and fire. Anyone in that room would have been killed." He turned back to Rogan. "Rogan, who did you anger?"

Daniel's hands paused for a moment as he sealed the evidence bag. That was a new thought, one that he had not had before. What if it was Rogan someone was after and using Tate to do so? Or was someone after the both of them?

Tag and Brownie exchanged glances with one another and then with their wives. They had discussed it among themselves and with others of their friends.

"Rogan?" Tate's voice was almost inaudible. "Is that possible?"

"It is, Tate. It very much is. I meet all kinds of people and there have been threats directed towards me, the shelter, and the mission. It's a given with what we do. So, yes, it is possible. I have not discussed this with Austin, but I intend to. Roger, you've repaired the fireplace."

"I have, Rogan, and checked out the water heater and furnace. They are fine. Just the fireplace. They would have gone for that as you won't have the furnace on yet and the water heater just wouldn't do what they wanted. It's used too much."

Rogan had paled as had Tate. That someone would tamper with their appliances had not crossed their minds. He was devastated at the thought of what could have happened if Tate had been on her own and decided to light it.

Austin had reappeared, a frown on his face. To be called back here for something like a tampered with fireplace was not what he had expected. He had heard the latter part of the conversation and stood for a moment beside Daniel who handed him the evidence bag.

"Roger?"

Roger pointed at the bag.

"That? That could have killed them or at the very least severely injured them. It was meant to do that. Find the people who did this." He walked away to set his tools back in his van and then pulled away.

Chapter 22

Late that evening, Tate wandered her home, feeling violated that someone had made their way into their home and endangered them. She could hear Rogan on the phone, a conference call with the board, he said. She sighed. So, who was this person actually after? Herself or Rogan? Tate had simply nodded as Ayron suggested that.

Rogan set his phone down. He had expected the response that he had received. The board had uttermost confidence in him and had told him that. Rogan had volunteered to step aside from the work until it was resolved but the board said no. They had no idea how long it would go on for and they couldn't just have Rogan stopping the work he was doing. They all said that with prayer, they had come to the united decision that Rogan should stay on. They would up the security there, without alarming the residents, and ensure that Tate had security with her as well.

Rising, Rogan headed for the kitchen, thinking that Tate would be there. Only she wasn't. He searched the house, finding her sitting on the side of the bed, arms wrapped around her abdomen, a woebegone look on her face. He simply sat beside her, an arm around her, not saying anything.

"Rogan? Did that really happen"

———

106

"It did, my love. I spoke with someone named Branigan and Joseph tonight. They are both heading our way tomorrow to install a security system here and at the shelter and mission. Branigan works for the Barnabas Foundation and is a security expert. Joseph is a security expert on a security team. They are both well trained and were available. They have worked together before."

"Okay. It just disturbs me that this has to happen. That these people invaded our home and did this to us. They really don't care about anyone's life."

"No, they don't. And it involves our neighbours now as well. A gas explosion may well have damaged other homes."

Tate stared at him, horrified at the thought.

"What do we do, Rogan? Move out to somewhere in the forest where there is no one around? Run and hide where they can't find us?"

"They would just find us, I think. We could try that. I would love nothing better than to take you somewhere safe and hide you there until this is all over. But it would only delay things, I suspect." Rogan grew thoughtful. "Austin called when you had stepped outside."

"He did? And?" Tate twisted to stare at him.

"He did. He didn't have a lot of information that he could share, but the summons was totally fake. He just doesn't understand why or who." Rogan stared down at Tate, watching the emotions flooding her face

"It was to get to me. I could have gone to that address and disappeared. So could you. What stopped me from running from the house?"

"God." Rogan paused for a moment, his thoughts on what might have happened to Tate and he shuddered. "God stopped you by allowing you to react as you did."

"He would do that, won't He? I am glad that I was stopped. Being with you has grounded me further into His word and His plans for me and for you. At one time, I would have fled the house and been taken. I know that."

"I am glad that you didn't. I would miss you greatly if you disappeared. Now, I'm going to lock up the house. I'm to stay home for the rest of the week, working from home I am told. Sunday, we'll have people around us at church. It will cause issues, I know, that I am not at the shelter, but the staff are good. If I am needed, I can go there. The board has arranged for security for both of us. We are not to be out anywhere on our own. Someone will be here at the house all the time. In fact, they have already started a twenty-four hour watch."

"The board would do that?" Tate was shocked and then nodded.

"They have, Tate. That's what they do. They call it being God's hands and feet on earth. They are concerned about both of u."

"So, where does this leave us? Where do we go then? We're putting people at risk. Has Austin found anyone at all?"

———

"Not yet, he hasn't. And for now, we go forward as we are, hand in hand, and with God watching over us. He has already walked this path before us."

"I see." Tate grew quiet, causing Rogan to turn his eyes to her. "Rogan? Can I ask a question?"

"You may." He waited patiently, knowing that she would ask when she was ready.

"Why did you become a preacher?" She turned to look at him, seeing his eyes steady on her.

"Why? I don't know if anyone has ever asked me that. I know Dad and I discussed it and he only asked if I had prayed about it and had peace that God has placed that in my heart to do just that. My grandfather on Dad's side was a missionary and Dad grew up on the mission field. I didn't have the feeling that was what I wanted to do, even though I had to fight it out with God and myself, telling Him that if that was where He wanted me, I was willing to do so. I have also been drawn into deep study of scriptures and felt I needed to pass on my thoughts and feelings and prayers. A regular church just didn't suit me. I have a burden for those who are homeless and alone."

"That's what everyone at the shelter and mission has said. That you are concerned about them to the point that you don't consider yourself. They worry about you, Rogan, that you will burn out. One person did say that he was worried about you being hurt, but when I asked what he meant, he simply shrugged and walked away. He really didn't say much about it."

“I see. I know who you mean. He did speak with me, but then he left town and I have no idea where he went.”

Chapter 23

Tate watched as the two men worked around her house the next day. Rogan had greeted them as friends, but she was hesitant about someone who she didn't know. Branigan and Joseph had greeted her with grins, explained what they were up to, and then just got to work. She had followed them for a bit before she headed for Rogan's office, to sit in front of his computer. There were books waiting for her to proof-read and she had no good excuse not to do her work.

Rogan had watched her closely from the doorway before he moved away. She needed this time, he thought, time to work and put aside what they were facing. He had watched the two men and then sent them down to the shelter and mission, knowing that their work was needed there as well, at least in the areas where Rogan worked. He had been in touch with the shelter and found that he would need to be there the next day.

Tate raised her head hours later, sitting back to rub at her eyes. She had caught a glimpse of Rogan moving around the office in the last half hour but had been almost finished the manuscript and had been determined to do just that. Tate frowned for a moment. What they were going through? It seemed like a plot in one of the manuscripts that she had read. Her fingers flying across the keyboard, she scrambled to search through her list of manuscripts, pausing at one. *This one,* she thought. *This one is just so like what we're going through. It's just been published but I wonder.* Tate sat back for a moment, hearing soft footsteps and then feeling Rogan pick her up and sit back down with her cuddled close to him.

Rogan's audible prayer calmed her. He then looked at her, his eyes on her face.

"What did you discover, my love? I know you have found something."

Tate turned her head, finding him almost nose to nose with her and then had him reaching to kiss her.

"This manuscript. It seems so much like what we're going through. Almost event by event. The only thing that we are missing are the photos, and I am sure that we will be getting them."

"A novel? Are you saying that someone is following a novel plot? That's an interesting supposition. Why would you think that?"

"I don't know. It just sounded so much like us. A homeless lady. A mission worker. Danger bringing them together. They didn't marry right away but he watched out for her. Just like you are doing. There was a bomb threat, not a real bomb like us. A tampered with gas stove, not a fireplace." Tate blinked, suddenly afraid. "If we tell anyone, they'll think it was me all along. That I trapped you into marriage for some reason and that I'll kill you." Tate began to shake in fear.

Rogan's arms tightened on her even as his eyes found the computer monitor and he read the synopsis for the novel. Tate was right. It sounded so much like what they were facing. Only how could it? Was someone following the plot line to destroy them for some reason? A reason that they didn't know? He reached for his email program, sending off an email to both Austin and Emma, adding the link, and what Tate had said.   Emma sent back a message immediately, simply stating that she had had a thought like that and was investigating that very novel.

Tate read her response, surprise on her face.

"How did she do that?"

"She can't explain it, my love. It's how her brain works.   She has a memory that defies explanation." He sat for a moment, his eyes on her face. "How be we find something for supper?"

Tate nodded, not really hungry. Her discovery had removed any appetite that she had.

"I guess. I'm not that hungry."

"I'm not either. How about just some soup or a sandwich?"

She nodded, up on her feet and away from him. Rogan's head dropped for a moment before he followed her, not quite sure what she was up to. Tate turned as he approached, not quite sure what to say. Her emotions were high, she knew, and she was ready for a confrontation and fight. Only, she knew Rogan would not fight her. He would simply hold her and pray.

Rogan sighed as his phone chimed. Now was not a good time for that to happen, but it had. He pulled it out, reading the text message. Austin had responded. Just where had that come from, he asked? And what did Tate mean?

Tate read the message and then simply took Rogan's phone from him. Her fingers flew over the keyboard as she responded. And then Rogan's arm was around her as they waited for Austin to respond.

"Tate? How do we explain this?"

Tate shrugged, her eyes focused on the wall in front of them. She frowned and then moved away, reaching for the photo.

"Rogan, this was not here yesterday. Who put this one here? It's different from the one you had." Fear flowed through her as he approached.

Rogan stared at her and then at the photo, before he reached for it. He sighed before he retrieved his phone from Tate and sent off a text to Austin. He read the response and turned to set the photo down. Reaching for Tate's hand, he tugged her with him to the office, sitting and pulling up the stream from their security system. There was nothing on it, which Tate simply stated meant that the photo had to have been placed prior to the security system installation. Who told on them about what they were up to?

Rogan stared at her, knowing what had not been done and needed to be done. He was on his feet, pulling her with him once more and then out of the house, locking her into his car despite her protests. Austin watched from where he had parked, not quite sure what Rogan was up to.

Rogan turned as he heard footsteps, anger on his face.

"Austin?   Was the house searched for anything?"

Austin paused, a hand rubbing at his face. He knew then what Rogan was asking.

"Not that I am aware of. That will be rectified immediately."

Chapter 24

Tate huddled down in a wicker chair on their front porch, her head on her upraised knees. They had not been allowed into the house and she wanted to know why. The crime scene techs had been around and then left. Austin was discussing something with his supervisor, and Tate wanted to know what. It concerned her after all and she just needed to know.

Rogan perched on the railing, one leg swinging as he gazed towards the street. He could see some neighbours milling around and he knew that he would need to speak with them. This was a close knit neighbourhood and each one looked out for the other.

Austin rubbed at his neck. To find what they had in the house was not what he had expected or wanted to see. How had this search not been done before? That was a question that he could not answer at the present time. He stood for a moment, his eyes closed as he prayed, hearing the sounds of nature in his ears, the night-time critters making their sounds and songs.

He walked back towards the house, his thoughts muddled for a moment, not like him at all. Why had this happened, he wondered? Who was this person really after? That he didn't know. Not any more. The photo? It was disturbing. The couple had not seen the writing on the back, that threatened them with death unless they did what they were asked.

Only, no one had asked anything of them. Was there more than one person involved? That was what the consensus now seemed to be.

"Austin?" Rogan watched as his friend paused on the steps before he moved to slump down into a matching wicker chair. "What can you tell us?"

Austin studied Rogan and then Tate. Something was off tonight but he was almost too tired to determine what.

"The photo had a threat on the back. Have you been asked to do something, either one of you?"

The couple shared a look, not sure of what Austin was asking.

"No, we haven't. Neither one of us. Is that what it said?"

"It did. I didn't think that you had but I had to ask. This is not looking good. Some will say that one of you planted the photo." His hand went up as Tate protested. "We know that you didn't. The handwriting is neither one of yours. As to the other search, we found some listening devices and some microphones. I suspect that they were planning on terrorizing you further. Did Branigan or Joseph do a search today?"

"No, they didn't. We didn't have a chance to discuss that. I suspect that if they had had any idea of that, they would have asked if they could." Rogan sighed. "Is the mission or shelter compromised?"

"I suspect not. That is too open and public a place for them to do so. In your home, they would have ample time and distance to listen in on what you were discussing. If you made any plans over the last few days, I would discard them. They are sure to be known." Austin gave a quick grin at Tate's disgruntled look.

"Okay, we can do that. We really didn't have any plans, just thoughts and ideas. Other than that plot line we seem to be following." Tate dropped her feet to the porch floor. "Now what do we do, Austin? I am not running and hiding. I've done enough running over the years. I want this over and over yesterday. We can't move on with our lives, Rogan can't continue with his ministry, and we can't be out in the open until it is."

"We understand that, Tate, and know somewhat of how you feel. We're trying, believe me, to find out who is behind this. Your mother still is not speaking with us. Someone has her terrified is what I'm being told."

"There is? I don't know about that. She never used to fear anyone. Who would do that do her, change her that much?"

Rogan stared at Austin, simply shaking his head. He had no idea what Tate was really meaning and would have to talk with her about that. Later tonight, he thought. Right now, we both have to process that someone was in our home, setting up devices that invaded our home and lives, and someone is asking something of us that we don't know what they want. That disturbed him more than he could say.

"Tate? What you said about your mom?" Rogan had tracked Tate down in his office, finding her looking for a book to read, after Austin had left. She had simply walked away from Austin's questions, refusing to answer any.

"What did I say?" Tate looked over her shoulder at him before her attention went back to the books and she pulled one from the shelf, opening it to leaf through it.

"That your mom was never scared of anyone. Did you mean that?"

Tate shrugged, not even sure herself what she meant

"I guess when you're a child, you see your parents and think that they aren't scared of anyone. I don't know that I can even tell you what I mean. It's more of an impression than anything else." She stared at the book, suddenly lifting it. "You see this book? It's a classic. But I have never read it. I have always wanted to but Mom told me I was not allowed to. Only she gave no reason for that. Why?"

Rogan approached, his hand out to tilt the book to read the title. He sighed to himself. There is no reason that Tate could not have read it.

"I'm sorry, Tate. I'm sorry that she said that. I'm sorry that you have not read it. What can I do or say to help?" He watched her closely, compassion on his face, even though he didn't understand why.

"I'm sorry, too, Rogan. I just don't know what to say. Not any more. Did Austin say anything more about her?" Tate was hopeful that he had but not really expecting that.

"It's my turn to say I'm sorry. He didn't. I'm not sure that he had any new information that he was able to share with you. Austin did say that they were in touch with the detectives where your mom was. They have put her somewhere that she can't be found."

"Is she in danger herself? Or is she a danger to me?" Tate looked up at Rogan, her mouth opening and then closing as she was unable to find any more words to express her thoughts.

Chapter 25

Unable to settle down to anything the next morning, Rogan paced the house and then paced the yard. He studied the grass and nodded. That was something he could do - mow the lawn and do the trimming. Working towards the back of the yard and the gardens there, Rogan paused. Something was off there and he wasn't sure what. He turned towards the house before he remembered that Tate was off with Rori, Keegan, and Ayron, for a ladies' day out. He smiled to himself. Tate had been excited to go but hesitant to put the ladies at risk. Rogan had simply hugged her, prayed for her, and sent her on her way. He knew that God was in control, no matter what happened.

Hearing a slight sound, Rogan spun in a circle, not quite sure what he had heard. He didn't see the man dropping over the fence before he was down on the ground, a baseball bat slamming into his ribs. Fighting to stay conscious, Rogan tried to move away, unable to avoid the second hit that caught his knee. The pain sent him spiralling down into darkness. He didn't feel the envelope dropped on his chest before the man was back over the fence and disappearing into the forest that lay there.

Cameron and Brownie had appeared at the front door, wanting to just pray with Rogan, sensing that he needed something like that. Brownie stepped back from the door, a frown on his face.

———

"He said he's been here. Keegan confirmed that with Tate. I wonder where he is." Brownie stepped away from the porch, Cameron following him. "Tate said that Rogan's parents were heading home from their vacation and were due in tomorrow. So he can't be with them."

"What about the back yard, Conor?" Cameron headed for the gate, intent on searching there.

"It could be. He may be doing work outside and not have heard us." Brownie followed his father, and then was running through the gate, heading for the back of the yard. "Call 911, Dad. We're needing them."

Brownie was on his knees, hands moving over Rogan, grimacing as the other man groaned and tried to move from his assessment. He turned as he felt his father's hand on his shoulder.

"Conor?"

"He's alive, Dad, but hurt. And I don't know how or who." Brownie moved away on Rogan and searched, even as his father watched the paramedics working on Rogan.

Cameron moved towards the house, knowing that he would only be in the way of the investigation. He watched from the back porch, his eyes not moving from Rogan. He was worried, he had to admit. This is not what they had expected to find, not at all.

Brownie moved towards his father, watching as the stretcher carrying Rogan was moved towards the street and then loaded. He drew a deep breath. Someone had to find Tate and he had no idea just where they were.

Cameron knew his son was trying to find the words to say what he had to.

"How bad, son?"

Brownie shook his head.

"I'm not sure, Dad. He is alive but as to his injuries? They can't say." He stared at his phone. "I need to find the ladies."

"Go and find them. I'll stay here for now. Someone has to lock up for Rogan." He took the keys that were extended to him. "Your mom will come and pick me up if I can't get a ride with an officer to the hospital."

"Thanks, Dad." Brownie was away, heading for the store that Keegan had just responded to his text with the name of where the ladies were. He wasn't ready for this, he thought. Not at all. Tate would be beside herself that she had not been home when this happened.

"Tate?" Keegan's hand stopped her forward movement along the sidewalk. "Brownie's here."

"He is? I thought that he was spending time with Rogan." Her face paled. "Rogan! He's been hurt." She almost ran towards Brownie, the other ladies trailing after her, exchanging worried looks. "Brownie?"

Brownie's hands stopped her forward rush.

"Rogan was hurt this morning, Tate. Come. Let me get you to the hospital."

Keegan's arm was around Tate, almost keeping her on her feet.

"Brownie's right. We'll get you there." She looked around, seeing Rori's fear and the worry on the other ladies' face. "Rori? You're with us?"

"I am. Let's move." Rori was worried about her brother but also his bride. She could see the absolute fear, no, terror, she thought, in Tate's face and movements.

Tate refused to sit as she waited in the Emergency department. Instead she stood near a wall, shifting from foot to foot, her eyes on the door that she wasn't allowed through yet. She could hear noise and voices around her but she didn't hear exactly what they were saying. Tate's whole attention was on her desperate wish to be where Rogan was and where she just wasn't allowed at the present time.

Rori watched Tate closely, standing beside her, an arm around her, feeling the other lady shifting on her feet. Her heart cried out for healing for both Rogan and Tate. This wasn't to have happened, she thought. She knew her parents were on their way but it would be a number of hours before they were in town. Tate needed her mother, a mother, and Rogan and Rori's would do.

Austin paused as he stepped through the automatic doors, searching for Tate. His eyes found her and he frowned. She should be sitting, he decided, but it didn't look as if she would. He headed for the doors, hearing a whimper behind him and knowing that Tate had moved closer. He shook his head at Brownie, knowing that Brownie would keep her there.

———

Chapter 26

Standing back from the stretcher, Austin watched the activity that surrounded Rogan. That man had not roused that Austin could see. He frowned again, trying to think through what he had been told. There had been no signs of the assailant and no one was sure how or when Rogan had been attacked.

Turning away, he pulled out his phone to check his text messages and voice mail. He knew that he would be there for a long while. Austin stepped away, walking through the ambulance bays to the outside, returning a call.

"Daniel? What do you have?"

"Whoever it was? It looks as if they came over the fence. Rogan not likely heard whoever it was as he had the lawn mower going."

"I wondered. There are traces of that?"

"There are. Footprints. Some fibres on the fence boards. The techs are working hard, trying to find everything they can." Daniel's voice died away. "They were watching him, Austin. We found spots where they were standing, where they could see the front and back yards."

"We wondered if they were doing that. Now we have confirmation of that." Austin grimaced as he looked around, feeling someone out there who was watching him. "They moved to the hospital, Daniel."

"That's a given. We knew that they would do that." Daniel's voice died away once more before he spoke. "Rogan? How is he?"

"They're still assessing him. They were waiting for imaging and blood work."

"And Tate?"

"She's not sitting down. I think Rori is trying to get her to do that but she's having none of it. I think she'll head in without permission if she gets a chance."

"They do need to be together. We'll manage that at some point." Austin turned as he heard footsteps. "Keep me updated, Daniel. I'll be back in the office at some point tonight. Brownie?"

Brownie stood, not answering, not really looking at anything. He had no words for how he felt or what he really wanted to say. This should not have happened and they still didn't know who the target was. Was it Rogan or Tate? Or someone else and they were using these two to bring a reign of terror to the family?

"Austin? How sure are we that Rogan or Tate are the actual targets?"

Austin stopped in his movement of tucking his phone away, his eyes on Brownie. His thoughts began to race. Was this the answer, Lord? The answer to what was puzzling them all?

"Why would you ask that?"

"It's just a thought. We've been brainstorming among ourselves, just trying to make sense of it all. And it isn't making sense. Tate can't give any answers as to why someone would be after her. Rogan? We know him. Unless it's something through the shelter or mission, we have no clue. And if there were issues that he didn't report, then he won't say. He won't break anyone's confidence."

"No, he won't." Austin turned to look back at the hospital. "Tate? Is she still standing?"

"No. Cameron convinced her to sit at last. She's wearing out, Austin. How do we end this? I know how it was for Keegan and me. It's draining to be under this."

"We understand that, Brownie. It's just that we don't have any answers, any hints. Nothing. Even your friend, Emma, is at a loss and I understand that's not like her."

"No, it's not." Brownie paused as Cameron walked to stand beside him. "Cameron?"

Cameron shook his head, worry and sorrow mingling on his face.

"Austin? How? Why? Do we have any answers?"

"Not yet. Has Rogan been awake?" Austin watched Cameron close.

"Not at all. That's concerning, but the physician said that is normal. They've brought in a surgeon to assess him. They're talking chest tube. Something about a collapsed lung?"

"I see. We wondered about that when we heard he was tender over the ribs. It's a temporary thing." Brownie watched the traffic moving around them, his eyes on a particular car that had parked near the entrance but that no one had exited. "Austin? That car? I've seen it around."

Austin turned slightly.

"I have too. Let's send their plate and see what happens."

Brownie watched the vehicle and its inhabitants before he turned and walked away. He needed space, he decided. Another good friend going through this? That hurt.

Austin watched the vehicles moving around him before he too walked away, this time back through the ambulance bays to the cubicle where Rogan lay. *This was not to have happened, Lord,* he simply stated. *But it has. Now, how do we solve this without anyone getting hurt worse? We are no closer to a solution and that scares me. We need to finish this for them, find out who it is and why. And I don't see that happening any time soon. We just don't have the information that we need.*

Chapter 27

Allowed back in with Rogan, Tate had almost run towards his stretcher. Her hand covered her mouth as she tried to stem the flow of tears. This she was unsuccessful in doing. She swiped angrily at them. Tate watched as Rogan just lay, not moving. It was evident that he was in deep pain, pain that she felt responsible for.

The physician stopped for a moment, his eyes on Tate before he walked toward her. The slight sound of his footsteps startled her and she jumped, her eyes huge as she turned to him. He smiled before he assessed Rogan once more. The imaging had been better than he expected and for that he was grateful.

"Tate? May I call you that?" At her nod, he waited, not sure if she would continue to speak. When she didn't he continued, the sound of the equipment and hurried movements in the hallway sounding in his ears. "It's better than we thought, Tate. Rogan has roused somewhat. His ribs are badly bruised and a couple of them cracked. Those will heal with time. We normally don't wrap them. At one point, we were not sure if the lung had been punctured but it hadn't."

"I see. God protected him. But the knee? What about that?" Tate's hand was on Rogan's face, her other hand rubbing at her own.

"The knee? There is some damage to it. Tendons and cartilage are torn. We watch it, Tate, to see how it heals and if it doesn't, then he'll face surgery. Rogan will need to wear a brace for now and for the first few weeks, he can't put any weight on it."

Tate nodded, not sure of what he was saying in its entirety but her only thought was that Rogan was alive and was coming home.

"When can I take him home?"

"He's rousing, so once he's awake and alert enough, we'll send him home." The physician hesitated, thinking that Tate would have more questions, but her attention was back on Rogan. He shook his head and walked away. There were other patients that needed his attention.

Rogan roused, his head twisting on the pillow as he did so. Squinting to try and get his bearings, he sighed. The hospital? Now what did I do, he wondered. My chest hurts and so does my knee.

"Rogan? You're awake? Please, Rogan. Look at me."

Tate's voice reached to him through the fog he felt that he was in and his head twisted once more. He watched as she swiped at the tears on her face. He sighed to himself. The pain was leaving him feeling like his head was in a fog and he had trouble focusing.

"Tate? Where am I?" Rogan began to shift on the bed, unable to find a comfortable position.

"You're in the hospital, Rogan. Please. You need to lie still." Tate was desperate to have him lie still. Only she was unable to make him do just that. "Please? Rogan!"

Rogan stared around once more, not taking in the equipment surrounding the bed or even the hospital room. He was afraid, he thought, so afraid. He didn't know what had happened. Rogan reached for Tate, finding her reaching for him in turn.

"Tate? What happened?" His voice was rough with the pain that he was in.

"You were attacked in our back yard. We don't have much information, Rogan. You were cutting the grass. Don't you remember?" Tate was desperate to hear that Rogan had recognized the attacker.

"I was? I don't remember. The last I remember is dinner. We have fish."

"That was last night, Rogan. You've forgotten a day." Tate stood back before she turned, searching for answers that might not come.

The physician stood, eyeing the paperwork in his hand. Rogan needed care and he wasn't sure that Tate would be able to provide that. She looks fragile, he thought. He walked towards them, drawing both sets of eyes towards them, one set pain-filled and one very apprehensive.

"Rogan? You're alert. Good. We're sending you home but I want you back in a week for more imaging, to assess the extent and healing of the knee."

"The knee? I don't understand?" Rogan pulled himself to a sitting position, pain evident in how he moved.

"You were hit in the knee. There is damage to tendons and cartilage that needs to heal. We're not seeing a fracture but that is always possible." The physician assessed him, seeing Rogan nod but not really understanding what was being said. "And you have bruised and cracked ribs. They will take up to six weeks to heal. You won't be weight bearing on that leg for a number of weeks and you will need to wear a brace for now. How you're going to manage? For now, you will be in a wheelchair. No options on that, Rogan. You can't manage crutches with the ribs."

Rogan nodded, sliding to sit on the side of the bed, an arm curled around his chest, almost bent over with the pain. Tate's arms were around him, afraid for him, not sure how they would manage.

Cameron and Brownie stood watching the couple before Brownie pushed forward the wheelchair.

"Ready to leave, Rogan?" His voice was quiet and taut, hiding his emotions.

"I am." Rogan drew a deep breath, his eyes on the hallway. He frowned. What was that man doing here? "Brownie? That man? Who is he? He's been hanging around lately."

Brownie shot a look behind him.

"I know him. He's a friend, Brownie, from some other town. He's wanting to speak with you, but he'll wait. He's left material for us to look over." Brownie's hand helped steady Rogan as he landed on one foot, his face contorting with the pain. "Here, let's get you into the chair and then home. Tate?"

"Yes, please, Brownie. I need to get him home. And God help me, I just don't know how we'll manage."

Cameron wrapped an arm around her, just as he would his own daughter, and walked her out following Rogan and Brownie.

"We'll help, Tate. That's a given. You'll have more help than you will need or want."

The man had followed them, waiting to speak with Brownie before he nodded and left, his head turning as he searched the area. Luke, a member of a security team, had been sent by his boss to find Rogan to warn him. Only, he wasn't in time.

Chapter 28

Late that night, Tate stood in front of the living room. The lights in the house were mostly off, other than the bedside light in the bedroom. They had managed to settle Rogan at last, much to his protest, and then the men had left, promising to be back in the morning. Cameron had watched Tate, seeing how tense she was and how much on the edge. His prayers had risen constantly for the young couple.

Rogan's father had called, having had a feeling that something was wrong. He had assured Tate that they were almost home. In fact, they would be home that night and would head their way in the morning. Would they be okay and could they manage for the night? Tate had stared at her phone and then answered that she thought she could. She just wasn't sure.

Heading through the house, Tate paused. Something was off, she thought, but it would wait until the morning. That had to be the case. Spinning as she heard a low tapping, Tate's hand went to her throat before she moved quietly through the house. Standing at the front door, she peeked through the window, seeing a young man with a flashlight illuminating his face. She drew a deep breath of relief. Reece was here but just how had that happened? He would tell her, that she was determined.

———

Pulling open the door, Tate simply stood, her arms wrapped around herself.

"Tate? Can I come in?" Reece moved her gently back from the door and closed it behind him. "Dad called. How is Rogan?"

"He's asleep, finally. The pain meds have kicked in. Did he tell you what happened?"

"He did. That Rogan was attacked and hurt. But you? How are you?" Reece watched his brother's beloved wife closely, seeing just how close to the edge she was.

Tate shrugged, not quite sure how to respond. If she started talking, she decided, she just might not stop.

Reece grinned at her before he turned her to the kitchen and seated her, the coffee pot turned on and tea in the process for Tate.

"About like that?" Reece set the tea in front of Tate and then sat across the table from her, his coffee mug in front of him. "Let me pray with you first, Tate, and then we'll talk. For a bit. You need to sleep."

"I know, but I don't know that I will." Tate's head went down on her folded arms, silent sobs shaking her body as Reece prayed for her.

Reece raised his head, then sipped at his coffee. He didn't know Tate, only knowing what Rogan and Rori had told him. He worked as an IT specialist for a small firm and had been travelling during the last month. Rogan had told him what was going on, but he had been skeptical. That was, until now. He could see the ravages of what she had been going through on Tate's face.

Tate raised her head, turning it as she heard a sound and then was gone, heading for Rogan. Rogan was restless and the only way to settle him, Tate found, was to crawl up beside him and just hold him.

Reece paced the kitchen. This was out of his league, he thought, not sure where he went or how he would help. Rogan was his older brother, his hero, his mentor. Even with five years between the brothers, they were close. Both had chosen their line of work, following their assurance from God that they were on their life path.

Rogan roused in the early morning, pain wracking his body. He drew in a ragged, deep breath, not sure what had happened, other than he hurt. His head moved and stopped as he stared at the wheelchair and then felt at his knee. Yep, he thought, a brace. So I have damaged that. And the ribs hurt a lot. His mind wandered back to the day before and he remembered the mowing and then the sudden attack. Unfortunately, he didn't remember the man. He vaguely remembered Brownie saying something about a letter but he had no idea what the contents were.

Shifting to the wheelchair, Rogan sat for a moment, his head hanging down as he breathed through the pain. Whoever it had been, they had hurt him and more than likely scared his bride beyond words. He wheeled to gather clean clothes and then towards another bathroom, pausing as he heard soft footsteps, fear in his mind for a moment.

"Rogan?" Reece stopped just feet short of his brother. He had spent the night in the spare room, knowing that Rogan would need help in the morning.

"Reece? When did you get here?" Rogan moved forward, his hand gripping at the wheels.

"Last night. Tate and I spoke." He reached for the clean clothes that Rogan had on his knee. "Let's get you cleaned up and then see how much you want for a meal."

Rogan nodded before he shifted to look back behind him.

"How was Tate last night?"

"She's terrified, Rogan, but thinking through what could have happened. She did say that Austin would be around this morning. He wants to get your statement and said for you not to say anything."

Rogan shook his head.

"That's odd. I gave it yesterday to an officer when I finally woke up. What does he mean?"

Tate turned from the counter to watch Rogan wheel towards her before she was beside him, on her knees, sobs shaking her body. He frowned, knowing that she didn't cry very easily. Reece studied the two and walked away. It was time, he thought, to call in friends. His phone out, he made that call and then walked away to let the couple have some privacy. His friend, Micah, an IT specialist on a security team and his friend, Branigan, from the Barnabas Foundation had promised to help. In fact, Micah said that he and his wife, Kat, were already working on this. They had planned on coming around with Luke

and Abi, another team member, later that day, if he
felt Rogan and Tate were up to it. Reece had simply
thanked them and commented that he would be there
as well.

Chapter 29

Rogan wheeled through the house around noon that day, frustrated beyond belief. He had spoken to the board chair and been assured that he could work from home as he needed to. He was to look after himself and Tate. That was what he had expected them to say but not what he wanted to hear.

Tate followed him, her arms wrapped around herself. She was scared, she had finally admitted, scared that Rogan would be killed and that it would be her fault. She was also terrified of harm coming to his family.

Reece turned from where he had seated himself at his brother's computer, researching, searching, trying to help. Only he didn't have much information to work with.

"Reece? Have you found anything yet?" Rogan stopped near the desk, looking around, feeling uncomfortable for a moment. He let something was off in the room.

"Not yet." Reece frowned as he looked over at his brother. "What's off in here?"

"I have no idea. Something is."

Tate shook her head, looking behind her as the doorbell rang. There wasn't supposed to be anyone coming in today, she thought, before she peeked out the door window and studied the two couples standing there.

"Can I help you?" She barely opened the door, bringing smiles to the faces in front of her.

"You're Tate. Reece described you well. I'm Kat. This is my husband, Micah, and Luke and Abi. Reece called in help."

"He did? I guess he did. I'm sorry, come on in. I'm not really aware of what is happening today."

Kat simply hugged her, feeling the shudders of fear moving through Tate's body.

"We went through some pretty bad stuff, Tate. We can understand to a certain extent what you are going through. God is there, even when it seems that He isn't."

Tate heard a man praying and realized that both men were praying for her and Rogan. It helped to ease her burden, knowing that there were ones here, standing beside her, who understood what was happening. She wiped at her eyes, tears not able to be contained.

"The men are in the office, Micah, Luke. It's down the hallway."

Reece stood there, reaching to greet his friends.

"This way, guys. I suspect that the ladies brought a meal for us."

Abi grinned at Reece, ease of old friendship on her face.

"We did. And we stopped at Rylee's Irish bakeshop."

"Oh, wonderful. I've been hungry for some of that baking."

Tate stared at the bags and boxes of food in front of her.

"You didn't have to."

"No, we did. It's what we do, Tate. We don't impose ourselves on others at mealtimes without contributing." Abi searched the cupboards for what she needed, her head tilting as she contemplated what she needed to say.

"That helps. Thank you, ladies." Tate stood, her hands gripping the chair back. "I just worry so much. And it seems as if someone may have been through our house. Rogan thought something was off in the office."

"Your security system was set?" Luke startled her as he spoke from beside her.

Tate shook her head

"No, no one set it after Rogan was removed. They didn't have the codes. I think Brownie may have asked but I didn't respond. I did this."

"No, you didn't. Whoever it is? They're the ones doing this. I understand from Rogan that you are not receiving what victims usually receive. That tells me whoever it is has been very close to you two."

"That's what we're told. We watch every day. Every. Single. Day. Not once have we seen anyone. I mean we think they've been close to the house, just the way there are disturbances in the garden. Not enough to be certain or to let anyone know."

Luke nodded.

"It's what they do. It's part of a technique that will be used to scare you and then make you look at everyone around you, suspecting everyone, even family members." Luke saw Tate turn to him, concentrating on what he was saying. "This is when they are dangerous. With letters, photos, that kind of stuff? It can be examined and possibly tracked. What they're doing? Nothing can be traced. Unless it shows up on your security cameras."

"And we've checked. We don't see anything. Rogan thinks that they sneak in when it's really dark and know where the cameras are, avoiding them."

"They're aware of what you have done for security. Joseph mentioned that he thought someone was watching you closely. He and Branigan searched your home when they were through but that was before yesterday." Luke turned, heading for Micah, who nodded, both men beginning their search.

Rogan watched for a moment before he turned his attention back to Reece.

"Reece, what have you found?"

"Not a lot. It's like Tate and her family didn't exist."

"That is strange. Someone is hiding this information." Rogan sat back, his eyes on the floor, as he thought it through. "I know Micah is searching but I know of someone who might be able to help. He's an ethical hacker but has become a good friend, a supporter of our mission." His phone was out as he searched his contacts and then sent off an email to his friend, Noah. "He's really busy but he usually responds in a short while."

"And Brownie and his friends are searching, aren't they?" Reece grinned at his brother for a moment.

"They are, as they can. It's frustrating, Reece, not knowing who. We can't prepare for anything that happens, not knowing who or why."

"That's what has us puzzled." Luke spoke from the doorway, a grim look on his face. "And Rogan, you were right. Someone was in here, I suspect yesterday with the confusion going on."

Rogan paled.

"An officer?"

Luke nodded

"That what Micah and I suspect. We need to talk to your police chief. Emma's been working on your case and she suspected this. Austin is clear, as is David. So for now, continue as you have been with them. Just watch what you say to anyone else."

"And Austin would have discussed this with his fellow detectives." Rogan's eyes slid closed, fear triumphing for a moment. As he felt Tate's hand on his shoulder, his arm swept around her. "How do we do this? And just where do we stand? I haven't had an update for days now and I need that."

Austin stood beside Micah, shaking his head. That was why he was there, and he suspected that neither Rogan or Tate would like what he had to say. The person who he had discovered involved in this?

A shelter board member who hated Rogan but tried his best to hide it.

Chapter 30

A week passed. Then another one. Tate struggled daily to keep her spirits up, to be bright and upbeat for Rogan just as he did for her. Then one day, it all crashed down on her. She stared at the envelope in front of her, an envelope addressed in her mother's handwriting. How had she found her and how did she know her married name and address? Tate spun in a circle, alone in the house for the moment. Reece had appeared to take Rogan for a medical appointment and had tried his best to persuade her to go with them, just shrugging when she refused.

A knock at the door startled her, and Tate spun that way, her hands clapped over her mouth to contain her scream. She crept on silent socked feet across the medium oak laminate floor, to stand near the door. A knock resounded again and she jumped. Her hand resting against the door, Tate raised herself on tiptoes to peek out and breathed a sigh of relief. Abi and Kat were there as well as a number of other ladies

"Kat? Abi? What is going on?" Tate hugged and was hugged by each lady. "What are you doing here?"

"We've come to help. Our guys are away and we wanted a road trip. We're not really that far apart, you know. You and Rogan need to come to our town." Abi grinned as she pointed behind her. "And

I brought Rylee, who brought lots of goodies from her bakeshop.”

Rylee grinned as she walked through to the kitchen, depositing boxes on the countertop

“And I did. I was told that there weren’t enough the last time. Grand and I baked lots, just for you.”

“What can I say but thank you.” Tate stared around at the ladies. “Introduce me, please. I assume from what you said the other day that they have all had problems?”

“We have. I’m Darci. I run an arts and crafts store but I used to be a forensics psychologist. I have done up a profile for you and Rogan, Tate, and have copies for you and for your detective. Emma also has it. Emma couldn’t make it today, but she said Abe and she would be around at some point.”

“Thank you. I was feeling so overwhelmed and disheartened today, and then God sent all of you.”

“That He did.” This was from a lady named Sarah. “I work as an electrician but needed a day off and away. This was a perfect opportunity. Now, let’s party for a bit and forget what you’re going through. If you don’t, you’ll wear out, Tate, and we can’t have that. Abi and Kat said that they shared our stories with you, so you know what we went through. We can give our own perspectives to help you, but each story is as individual as the persons involved.”

“That’s correct.” Elizabeth spoke up. “It was with each of us. But one thing that we all had was not just the support of our fellows and friends, but we knew that God was in control. That He allowed what we faced for a reason, whatever that may have been."

Murphy's Adriel was nodding.

"Murphy always maintains that God has a plan and purpose that He may not have shared with us as yet. Sometimes, we don't know why we face what we do, and we may not until we face God in heaven."

"That's what I'm struggling with, I guess. I mean, Rogan is a preacher and is able to give me all these verses that help. We pray constantly for one another and for those involved in this, but there is always a sense that something big is about to happen. That scares me."

"We understand that so well, Tate." Leah moved in to hug her. "And we will cover you and Rogan with prayer. We have been doing that. But first, what can we do for you? I understand that you were just moving into an apartment when this all happened and not likely had a lot of things."

"No, I never had have. Rori and her mom have helped that way as have other friends of Rogan. It's just so hard. I don't want a lot or need a lot. At least, I don't think that I do."

"You have what you need, right? Okay. Then, this is what we do. We don't go out shopping for you for things. We look for what will help you cope and get through this." Lydia spoke up. "I work with my Dad's mission and we go into where there have been disasters to provide emergency supplies. I get what you're saying, Tate." She looked around. "Now, let's eat and then do some praying and then some planning."

The ladies agreed, milling around the kitchen before heading for the back deck, exclamations coming from them as they saw the area that Rogan and Tate had been working on. Rogan had simply stated that their backyard was their oasis, their hideaway spot, and they need it to reflect both of them.

Tate locked the door late that afternoon. Rogan had appeared a couple of hours earlier, greets the ladies, hugged Tate, and then headed back into the house. She had not heard how his medical appointment went, Reece simply shaking his head at her. Standing beside the couch, Tate stared down at Rogan, before she was on the floor, her arm wrapped around her sleeping groom, her head buried against him. She was unable to control the sobs, despite her best efforts. Exhausted, she too slept, not feeling Rogan rouse and then reach to draw her up beside him, despite the pain that cause him.

Rogan stared across the room, his focus on his fireplace. Reece and he had had a good long talk that morning, finding a spot in a local cafe for coffee after his appointment. Reece had forwarded emails that he had been receiving from friends with suggestions and proof of what was going on. Rogan had been dumbfounded, to say the least, to see who had been suggested.

"It can't be him, Reece. There's just no way." Rogan had been adamant that it was not the board member everyone seemed to suspect.

"I think it is, Rogan. I've watched him over the years. He's changed. Changed towards you. Change towards the mission and shelter. Changed towards the people you are helping. He's giving off something with his words and actions that no longer ring true to what the board stands for."

"He is? I've never seen that. But then, come to think of it, he really hasn't been talking to me much lately. And if that's why?"

"That could easily be it. If he saw you and Tate together, just talking, he might have made plans to get rid of you and bring in someone of his own. And you haven't resigned. You can be sure that he will continue to try and force you out." Reece was troubled for his brother, not quite sure what he faced.

"I see. Then, we must do everything we can to prove him wrong." Rogan sat back, studying his younger brother. "And you have a plan."

Reece grinned and nodded.

"In those emails are plans that we have all come up with as well as ways and means to keep you two as safe as we can."

Chapter 31

Tate sorted through the paperwork that had been left that afternoon and then sighed. She sank into a chair in the office, reaching for a pad of paper and pen, determined to make some sort of sense of it all. She forgot about the time, just working away. She vaguely heard the sounds of Rogan moving around the house, the slight squeak of his wheelchair letting her know that. Tate thought that she had heard both Reece and Rori but was not even sure of that.

Rogan paused in the doorway, turning his head slightly to stare behind him before he turned back to Tate. He moved forward, gentle hands reaching for the papers that Tate was holding. He knew that she wasn't concentrating on him but on what she had read.

"Talk to me, Tate. What did you discover?"

"I'm not sure." Tate sat back, a puzzled look on her face. "Who's here?"

"Just us. Austin was through and took what Micah and Luke found. And they found stuff as he so eloquently called it."

"They did? When was it placed?"

"Likely when I was hurt and the house was locked up without the security system being set. He'll look into that." Rogan studied the papers, flipping through them. "You've done a lot."

"I guess. I just want this over." Tate leaned against him. "You haven't said what the doctor said. We haven't had a chance to talk."

"No, we haven't. Listen. I know neither of us feel like eating but Rori left some grilled chicken and a tossed salad. Let's eat and talk at the same time."

Tate nodded, rose, and then paused.

"There is something in all this, Rogan. I'm just not seeing it."

"We'll work it through. In fact, we've both been working on this all day. Let's set it aside for the evening and pick it up fresh in the morning. I have to do some work for the mission in the morning, but we'll make time for this."

Tate nodded, her eyes on Rogan.

"Rogan? Abi told me that it will only get worse from here on out. Is that what you're sensing?"

"I think it is. God has us, Tate, no matter what happens."

"I get that, but it still scares me."

Early the next morning, Tate was on her feet, dressed and heading for the kitchen. A cup of tea in hand, she reached for her Bible and then headed for the office. Sinking into a chair, the cup of tea hit the table and her Bible was open as she searched for anything that would bring comfort.

An hour later, she reached for the paperwork that Rogan had taken from her the night before. There had to be an answer in here. The chiming of her phone drew Tate's attention. She smiled at the messages of support and prayer that she was receiving and then opened her emails. Yes, the ladies had been busy, as had their fellows. Tate frowned as she read the emails and their attachments, rising to her feet to head for the printer and print off the documents. Rogan would need to see them, she decided. She would not let Austin have them as yet. They had been sent to her.

Rogan paused in the kitchen, his head turning as he heard Tate moving around the office. He sighed. He wanted this over. He wanted to be able to take Tate out on dates and for walks and just live their lives and they couldn't.

"Rogan? You're up!" Tate moved into his hug and his kiss, content to just stand and be held.

"I am. You've been up for a while." He squinted at the clock. "It's only 7 in the morning."

"I know. I couldn't sleep. I spent some time searching for verses to help us. And the ladies and fellows from yesterday have been busy. They have emailed all sorts of information. I printed it."

"To give to Austin?" Rogan frowned as she shook her head.

"No. Not right now. It's been sent to us. We need to go through it." Tate shrugged as he continued to stare at her.

"Okay. But we'll need to at some point."

"We will. Your friends from here?"

"My friends from here? What about them"

"Can we get together with them? Go through this. Only that puts Brownie at a conflict of interest."

"Not necessarily. He's not the investigating officer. And this is only information that hasn't been proven. I'll talk to him and have him talk to his supervisor and clear it." Rogan tightened his hold on her. "What made you ask for them?"

Tate shrugged once more.

"I don't know. We need people who know the area and the people. I just thought.." Her voice died away. "Maybe this isn't such a good idea after all."

"It is. I'll call them. In fact, Shay sent a message last night that they were all off today. Did we want company?"

"They are? Okay, then." Tate stood for a moment, lost in thought. "Rogan, where's your wheelchair? You're on your feet."

"I know. I can go without it now. The surgeon says I am healing much better than he thought I would. I told him that was God at work."

Chapter 32

Tag and Shay stood two hours later, staring at Tate as she continued to thrust piles of paper at her. Tag's eyes raised and he smiled as he saw the paperwork lining the walls of the office and spilling out into the dining room.

"You're prepared, Tate." He grinned at her as she nodded enthusiastically.

"I am. I have reams of papers for us to go through. I suggest that we split it. I've organized it by person, by date, by location, by event."

"Well organized." Evan reached for the paperwork. "We'll go through it and then one of you ladies can scribe the walls for us." He grinned as her frown before her face brightened.

"That's exactly what we do." She spun and then was back in front of them. "I heard of a man who used logic problems to solve mysteries like this. We need to do one. I love solving them." She was away before any of them could respond.

Shay gave a laugh.

"She's determined to solve this today if we can. Let's see how far we can get." He moved away, reaching for another pile of papers.

"Shay's right." Evan moved away as well, heading for Brownie and Storm. "Storm, you've been around this area as has Shay. You know the undercurrents here. What are your thoughts?"

Storm turned, his eyes thoughtful.

"I have been. Rogan mentioned that a board member was involved. I would say yes, but not just him. This has gone on for far longer than we know. Emma's sent paperwork and details of who and why and when it all started." He shot a look towards the door, breathing a sigh of relief when he didn't see Tate. "That man? A second cousin to her father. We need to look at how he died once more. And then see why her mother has been on the run for so long. What ten years or more?"

"Around that." Brownie sat on the edge of the desk, arms folded across his chest. "Tate has admitted that she would think that she would see her mother in the towns that she lived in. As to why she moved? She was restless, not knowing why. She didn't feel as if she had a home any more. She has also said that her mother gave away everything she owned and most of what Tate owned before she disappeared. That hurt Tate more than she'll admit to."

"That's so sad." Breckon had approached with a tray of coffee, Shay's arm going out to hug her to him. "I can't imagine life like that. Flannery would know what it's like."

"Flannery and Tate have spoken." Evan looked towards the door. "Flannery hasn't said what about and only will if Tate agrees that she can, but she is always saddened after their calls. It brings back her own life on the streets."

"That it would. Breckon? You've spoken with Tate?" Tag searched the lady's face.

"I have. And I won't say what about, only that she has opened up more and more towards me and the other ladies. She has never really had a friend, not a close one, all of her life. She feels devastated that she has had no one. We need to stay close to them, Shay." Tears sparkled in her eyes.

"And we will. Now, about this material? You ladies are working through some." Shay simply swept his wife into a hug, his eyes on her face, saddened at the thought of Tate having no one that she could depend on.

"We are. We're working on what Tate faced in the towns that she lived in, what she thought, who she might have seen. That sort of stuff." Breckon moved away, leaving silence in her wake. The men watched before exchanging glances and then reaching for the piles of paper.

Flannery raised her head for a moment, a finger marking her spot.

"Tate? This last town that you were in? What made you leave it?"

Tate looked up, surprise on her face.

"That town? Edgeton? I don't really know. I just didn't feel at home there, I guess. I had been looking for a town that I could settle into and this just wasn't it. There was something evil around me there, I always felt. I can't explain it. I would find my room disturbed when I would go home. I was renting a room at that point. It would seem to be searched. I would ask the landlady and she couldn't explain it."

"Let me have her name." Keegan reached for her pen. "We'll look into her." At the name, her hand froze. Unknown to Tate, this lady was related to that person on the board, a former sister-in-law. That was a connection that they hadn't know about. "Tate? What do you know about your other's family?"

Tate turned to look at her, her mug of tea suspended in the air before she sipped at it. She thought through what she knew about his family.

"Not a lot. I was so young when he died. Mom got rid of everything about him that she could. I only knew his name and how he died. She never talked of him at all." Tate stared around at the ladies. "Kat was working on that, she said yesterday." Tate blew out a breath, frustration evident. "I wish I had pushed it more, but she would just tell me to stop and then walk away."

"That's sad, Tate." Breckon reached to hug her. "Dad said he and Shay would work through this as well. He's an investigator."

Tate turned to watch her and then the other ladies, finding them all watching her in turn. There was no censure or hatred. Instead, she could feel the concern and love from her friends. They were modelling Christ-like behaviour in how they reacted to her.

"Thank you, ladies. This definitely helps. We have so many working on this, we should solve it soon." Tate looked down, blinking away tears.

Chapter 33

Rogan walked through the house, his leg paining him. He had not rested that day as he should have, desperate as he was to try and solve what was going on. It had not been easy to hear that a board member was suspected, although that had been hinted at before. To hear that it might involve Tate's father? That had been a difficult pill to swallow.

His head tilting, Rogan smiled. Tate was singing to herself as she tidied up the kitchen, neatly stacking the paperwork in the order that they had left it. She was troubled, he knew, and he had no way of knowing how to comfort her, other than to pray for her and to hold her as she wept.

Tate turned, a smile on her face. She had come to terms with the information that had been unearthed that day. Her father? He was a figure in her life but she didn't know him, so whatever was dug up? It might affect her but it would not destroy her. She just wanted to speak with her mother, to find out why she had refused to talk about him.

Rogan stood for a moment, balancing awkwardly for a moment, before he spoke.

"Did we accomplish anything in the last couple of days?"

Tate frowned and then gave a small smile. She moved past him to study the papers on the walls.

———

"I think we did. There is just so much there that we need to process. How do we get this condensed and to Austin?"

"We don't." Rogan's finger laid against her lips, stilling her protest. "We let him know what we have. He'll come and take a look at it, take what he needs, and work from there. Emma has sent him information as well. I'm not sure how much or if it is the same as what we have. I would suspect that he has the same. She'll have verified everything before she has done that."

"I know that she will have." Tate hugged him, needing that contact with him. "I fear for us, my love. It's getting so hard to live."

"It is, Tate. Just know that I love you so much, more and more each day. I want this over. We need to go on with our lives and we can't."

"We can, Rogan. Our friends have, despite the danger and fear that they faced." Tate leaned back to look at him. "I love you too." She stepped back, her hands in his. "As you said last night, we leave this for the night. We need to spend time in prayer and petition."

"That we do. This is where it gets dangerous, sweetheart. Now, let's eat and then head for our oasis. We need to find that place of peace."

Tate nodded as she turned to walk away. Rogan's head dropped as intense fear swept through him. The men had all warned him that going forward, knowing what he did, that he would be in even more danger than they had been. The items that they hadn't been receiving? The photos. The packages.

The footsteps following them. The potential assaults and abductions. They would come and come hard and fast. Rogan's fear became almost palpable before he began to petition the heavens for help and comfort and relief. He felt God's peace there, knowing that he was never alone. God had promised never to leave him or forsake him. That brought some comfort to him. But in his humanness, he still feared for his love.

Tate snuggled down beside Rogan, his arm around her, as he set the glider on the back deck into motion. He had never thought to purchase one but had gladly done so when Tate had looked longingly at one a few weeks prior. It had become a favourite spot for them to end their day. Their prayer corner, Tate liked to call it. But what would they do in the wintertime? She had smirked at him that day when she asked him that. He had simply grinned and said that it would fit into his office. Would that do?

Rogan raised his head in the middle of the night. He wasn't hearing things, he thought. There is someone outside their home. He rose, dressing quickly, a hand out to waken Tate. A finger to her lips, he quietly asked her to dress. Someone was outside and they needed to be ready to run.

"But you can't!" Tate was reaching for her clothes, dressing as rapidly as she could. "But they can't get in. Can they?"

"They shouldn't be able to. Not with the security system that was set up. But they could be in and out before anyone could get her."

Tate muffled her scream as she heard a window break, spinning to see where it was. Rogan reached for her hand and pulled her into the bathroom, locking the door. He motioned without words to the window and they slipped through. The jar of landing sent pain through Rogan's body before he grasped her hand and pulled her with him, towards the neighbour's yard.

They slid to a halt behind the garden shed, their eyes on each other before Rogan peeked around the edge. They could hear their security system sounding in a shrill manner before they saw three figures running away, one towards them, the others towards the back of their yard. Rogan shoved Tate further into the darkness and then down to the ground, covering her body with his. They waited, not sure if they should rise or not.

They heard the sirens of the approaching patrol vehicles and raised their heads, ready to move before Rogan froze in his movements. He felt the poke of a weapon in his back and groaned. They were found. Hauled to his feet, Rogan's hands were bound behind him. He heard the whimper from Tate as she was too bound and then shoved forward. *Lord, I have no idea who these are or where we're heading. But You do. You are in control. You will protect us. If it is Your will that we survive, thank You. If it is Your will that we come home, that is Your plan for us.*

Chapter 34

Austin stood on the driveway of Rogan and Tate's house, his head tilted as he listened to the young female patrol officer. He grimaced, knowing that what they had feared had happened.

"There is no sign of them?"

She shook her head.

"The bathroom window in the master suite is open. It looks as if they made it out. Dag is bringing in Titan to search."

"Good. All right. You can go back on patrol. Just make sure I get what information you have."

"I will, Austin. I'm sorry that we didn't make it in time."

Austin nodded, knowing that even if a patrol vehicle had been on that street, it not likely would have made much difference.

Brownie walked towards him, to stand staring at the house.

"Did they get away?"

"They got out of the house but we don't know where they are. The officers are searching. Dag's heading in with Titan."

Brownie nodded, his eyes searching before he pointed.

"That way.   That leads from the master bedroom." He walked that way, Austin keeping step with him. "That shed? A hiding spot?"

Austin's large flashlight searched, finding multiple footsteps. His hand stopped Brownie's forward step.

"No, Brownie. We need the techs. There are footprints here, more than Rogan and Tate's."

Brownie sighed, knowing that Austin was correct. Rogan and Tate had disappeared.

"We were working with the others yesterday. There were ladies here from Riverville the day before. You may want to take a look at the papers on the walls and see what they determined."

"They were, were they? And what conclusion did you all come to?"

"Did you know that board member is distantly related to Tate's father?"

Austin's hand froze as he rubbed at his neck. That was something that he had not been aware of.

"She is? That changes it, doesn't it?"

"That's our question.   Who are they after? Rogan or Tate? Or both? Has she been chased to this town, to the shelter, to meet with Rogan? Only it wasn't planned that they married?"

Austin stared at Brownie, his thoughts tumbling over one another.

"What did you just ask?"

Brownie's look was shuttered. His thoughts too were troubled.

"What if they weren't to marry? And this has thrown a monkey wrench into their plans? The plans have had to be changed and that was why they haven't been approached or threatened more than they have been."

Austin's hand gripped Brownie's arm as he tugged him back towards the house.

"I need to see what you have come up with. Is it on a PDF file?"

"Not that I am aware of. Tate talked about that, but I don't think they had time to do that. Rogan was adamant that she would not work on that last night. He felt that they needed a break from it all."

Austin wandered along the walls of the rooms, his phone out as he took pictures of each paper. They are good, he thought. Organized. Well thought out. Structured. The questions and answers that were available are here. What have we missed in our investigation?

Brownie watched before he approached Austin, a stack of envelopes in his hands.

"These are for you. I forgot to grab them last night when I left. Can you take them now or not?"

"They've been logged into evidence?" At Brownie's nod, he sighed. "I can. Let the techs take them and I'll grab them from there." He pointed at a name. "Who is this? I don't recognize that name."

"That name?" Brownie frowned. "I don't know that I was told. That's Tag's handwriting."

"Okay, I'll talk with him." He looked around as he heard the dog's nails sounding on the wooden floor. "Dag?"

"We tracked them to the shed next door, just as you thought. Titan tracked them to the street behind and then the scent disappears. I'm sorry, Austin. I don't have any more information to share." Dag was frustrated and angry.

"Thanks, Dag. You and Titan have done the best that you two could. Head off and get me your report."

Chapter 35

Two days went by and then another two. Reuben and Rosa were around as were Rori and Reece. It had devastated all of Rogan's family that the couple had disappeared. They had felt the younger ones should have been safe in their home, a security system in place. Why had they been taken? And just who had done that?

Reuben searched the town. A retired police officer himself, he knew just what the couple would face. He feared for their lives. His attention went to the shelter, the only known common bond between them. Reece and he had taken their own photos of the papers on the wall, working through it. Reece had set up a database, entering the information and trying to search for something common in it all. He wasn't liking what he was finding and told his father bluntly that someone at the shelter had to be involved.

Rori had wept and then met with the ladies in the area, determined to come to a conclusion and find her brother and his bride. None of them were able to. The couple seemed to have disappeared into thin air.

The shelter board had met, one of the members very vocal about having Rogan removed. Instead, he was removed and a new member was installed. Tag had been appointed to fill the term remaining. His friends had looked at him and then nodded. Their consensus was that this would help. That he would be able to assess the remaining board members and determine if any one else was involved.

The removed board member was angry beyond anything that he had ever experienced. He wanted Rogan and Tate to pay for his removal. Only he had no idea where they were. The men he had hired? They were not responsible for removing them from town. They had searched a well but to no avail. The couple had simply vanished.

Austin was exhausted. He was wearing thin working on all the cases that suddenly appeared. The same could be said of all the other detectives. They were frustrated to say the least, knowing that a friend was missing and unable to find him. Rogan had made himself available for the detectives to talk with, to seek advice from when they were in need of that. He had listened, given advice, and then checked in with them on a weekly basis, his prayers appreciated even for those who claimed to have no faith. He had been a minister, a preacher to them without forcing them to change to what he believed. When questioned, Rogan had simply smiled and said that he was called to be the hands and feet of God on earth and that meant he ministered to everyone.

Walking back around the house, Austin studied it and then the yard. Something had brought him back that day, but just what that was, he wasn't even sure. He just had to come. He walked the yard and then heard a voice calling to him.

Rogan's neighbour, Bill Waite, was walking towards him, a hand out to shake his.

"Austin? You're back around?"

"I am. I know that you have talked with us. Anything else that you can tell me?"

Bill nodded, and then pointed back to his patio.

"Come and sit. It's lunchtime. Let's eat and then we'll talk. I have information that I just discovered today or rather was told and that I need to give to you. But first, you need to be refreshed."

"Thank you, Bill. I do appreciate that. I know that you and the other neighbours have been keeping an eye out for Rogan and Tate. That's appreciated."

"I know." Bill sat back from his lunch, trouble on his face. "Austin, what I have to tell you is second-hand to me. Someone on the street reached out to me. A young man who is afraid for his life if you approach him."

"I see. We have undercover officers that can approach him if necessary."

"No, that won't work. He's afraid to talk to anyone. How he reached me, I can explain at some point but for now, let's leave it." Bill rubbed at the patio table, brushing off crumbs from his sandwich. "I guess if I just talk and then you can ask questions."

"Sounds fair." Austin's notepad was out as was his pen. "Just talk and we'll discuss it." He waited before his head was bowed and he was praying.

"So, Austin, this young man approached me this morning as I was fishing in the river not far from here. He kept his distance, pretending just to sit and watch the river flow. He is concerned about Rogan. Rogan has been there for him, helping him to finish his high schooling, and plan for college. He was

---

168

researching grants and scholarships for him. Apparently this young man was reading in the library one day when he overheard a couple of men and a woman talking. When Rogan was named, he began to listen harder. He did take notes, which he left for me this morning. I will pass them on to you. At the moment, I have them locked away in my safe.

"Anyway, this trio was talking about how to get to Rogan. They had planned to forge his signature on cheques from the shelter and let him face embezzlement charges. They also planned to have him charged with child endangerment charges. Just what those were, they weren't clear in this conversation. They mean him harm, Austin. Only they have no idea where he is. When he and Tate married, that changed what they had planned and those plans now included charges against her."

"That's what we were thinking. Bill, what else?"

"This is concerning, Austin. I have no idea where they are. We need to find them. I looked around the shed. Someone has been back around, searching for what, I have no idea."

"That's fair to say." Austin studied the shed and then the land behind it. "Your property backs onto a farmer's field. That's where they were taken through. Our dogs tracked them that way."

"I know. Kids like to run through here and hide in the fields. We're planning on fencing it off. Maybe it would have been different if we had already done that."

"Not likely. They would have found a way to get them away." Austin studied his notes, a puzzled frown n his face. "I need to speak with this young man at some point."

"And he will. Right now, he won't. If you search for him, he has said he'll run. And I don't want that to happen."

"No, we don't want that."

Austin rose at last, walking back to the shed, staring at it and then at the fields behind it. There had to be an answer somewhere. Only he had no idea what that was.

Chapter 36

Running for his vehicle, Austin slid behind the wheel, reaching for a towel to rub at the rain on his hair. The rain had been heavy all day and the winds were picking up. This was not what he had planned on, that was for certain. It was to have been his day off but he had been called in to a case conference about one of his cases, one that involved other towns. Austin had sat through the meeting, listening and taking notes, when something said had triggered an idea. He had been impatient for the meeting to end and when it was, Austin had headed for his vehicle and home.

He paced his office as he waited for his coffee to brew and then with the largest cup he had filled full, he headed for his office. Sighing as he sat, Austin stared at his desk before he reached to wake up his computer. He had an idea of who was all involved but didn't have the proof. That he needed to find.

Daniel came looking for him, a package in his hands.

"Austin? I found this at Rogan's when I stopped by on patrol. It's addressed to you."

"What's that?" Austin pulled his attention back to the present. "What is that?"

"A package. Addressed to you. And I found it at Rogan's."

"At Rogan's? For me? That's bizarre." Austin reached for it, studying the addressing on hit. "I don't recognize the writing. Find one of the techs for me." He looked up. "Jayne? You're here?"

Jayne, one of the crime scene techs, nodded.

"Daniel called for one of us. Here. Let me take it and do what I need to." Jayne had the package and was gone before Austin could say anything.

Daniel sat in front of Austin's desk, a puzzled look on his face.

"I don't get it, Austin. Why leave something there?"

"I was around there a day or so ago. Just trying to get a sense of what happened and where they are. There's a large field behind them."

"I know. Rogan likes being on the edge of the country as he calls it but at this time, it left an escape route that we couldn't track very well." Daniel looked up at Austin. "What's your take on all this?"

"It's strange, I must admit. We have had no word on them. No ransom notes. This has seemed off all the time. Rogan says that they haven't been receiving all the normal "stuff" as he calls it that victims usually do."

"That's what he said. Now, this package? I don't get why leave it there."

"Someone has been watching his friends and us. They know that we patrol there regularly and that one of us walks around the house every few days. Whoever it is? They must have thought it was a safe place to leave it and that we would find it at some point." He looked up as Jayne reappeared. "Jayne?"

"Austin? What are you and Rogan mixed up in?" She handed over the evidence bags. "This just seems too strange."

Austin reached for the bags, his eyes on Jayne before he looked down, a frown appearing on his face. He studied each bag, laying each one down on the desktop.

"This is strange. Rogan's watch. Tate's bracelet. Photos of them in a well-decorated room. They don't look as if they have been hurt, but there is something off about that. A photo of their home. One of the shelter. But no note?"

"No note. Nothing to explain why. Unless there is something hidden in the photos." Jayne reached for the photo of the house. "There is something off about this, Austin. I'm not familiar with his house."

Austin reached for the photo, his eyes on Jayne and then on Daniel. Then they dropped to the photo. He studied it and then was on his feet. There was something there after all.

"Thanks, Jayne. You've helped. Daniel, you're with me." Austin almost ran from his office, the door locked behind him.

His vehicle screeching to a halt on the street at Rogan's home, Austin's door slammed behind him as he was out of it and running for the front of the house. He searched the photo and then the porch, heading for one of the shutters. Daniel was beside him, gloves on his hands as he reached for the tip of an envelope that showed from behind that very shutter. The envelope pulled out, the men studied it, puzzled once more that it was addressed to Austin. They felt as if someone was playing a game with them.

Austin carefully slit the envelope and pulled out the letter, his heart in his mouth. He recognized Rogan's handwriting. This was not what he had expected to find.

"Austin?" Daniel was reading over his shoulder. "Is this for real?"

"I don't know." Austin reread the letter. "Austin, if you are reading this, Tate and I are safe but it is not safe enough for us to come home. We know who is behind it all, but we can't prove it. The person who is helping us has left that package for you. If you search the photos carefully, you will find what you need to find the persons responsible. If you need to reach us, just leave a note on the community board at the library. It will be checked daily. And yes, we are safe and well. We can't go into any more details at present. Rogan."

"This doesn't make sense. Who took them? The person Rogan mentions?" Daniel searched the porch and then looked over the railing into the garden. "The rain will have removed any trace of evidence."

"It will have." Austin was distracted by the note. His eyes searched the area, finding nothing. "Let's head back to the office. I want you working with me. I'll clear it with your supervisor."

"Good. I need to do this." Daniel fastened his seat belt, staring at the house. "Who would do this? It's not making sense."

Austin nodded, his fingers tapping on the steering wheel, not quite sure where he went or what he did. *Lord, it would be really great if You cleared things up for me right about now. It's not making sense and that means they are still at risk.*

Chapter 37

Three days later, Austin was still puzzled by the information that he had been provided with. He had had to set it aside, other cases taking precedent over this one. He was frustrated, very much so, and headed out of the office to walk the streets. He looked up to see Brownie, Tag, Evan, Shay, and Storm heading his way. And walking rapidly across the street, another friend named Dougal. The gang is all here, he thought.

"Guys?" Austin stopped. "You're all here?"

"We are. We're determined to find them and find them today. We know who has them, Austin." Shay was adamant about that.

"I see. Okay, so where are you meeting?" Austin turned in a circle, feeling eyes watching them. "We need to get off the street."

"We do. Head for my place. I have everything there that I need." Brownie spun and walked away, anger in his movements. Anger not at his friends but at whoever it was that had led Rogan and Tate to danger.

Gathered in Brownie's office, the men sorted through the documents and then began to read, pads of paper and pens deployed to good use. Quiet conversation was heard among the sounds of rustling paper and scratching pens.

Dougal looked up. He had been a patrol officer for years and had gone through an adventure as it was termed. He feared for his friend.

"So, this man on the board? How is he related to Tate?"

"Cousins of a sort, if I remember." Shay looked up. "Tate really doesn't know her paternal side of the family or any history. She simply stated that her mother got rid of everything related to her father and never spoke about him. Tate didn't want to stir up anything by asking and when she reached a certain age, she just couldn't be bothered."

"I can see that. She hides a lot inside." Tag looked around. "Where did we leave that family tree Kat provided for her family?"

"Right here." Evan looked at it as he reached to hand it over and then pulled his hand back. "This isn't good."

"What isn't good?" Storm looked around from where he had been researching on the computer.

"This. Her family tree. They're really connected to this town. One of the founders in fact. A paternal grandfather way back."

"What?" Austin stared at Evan before he reached for it. "This is what we've missed. This link. So where does it now lead us?"

"Down a new rabbit hole." Tag was reading back through his notes. "It was rumoured when this first started but there wasn't any credence given to it. So, we set it aside for now." He searched through the stack of papers in his hand. "Here. Emma has information on it. She sent it last night along with more information from Kat, such as they are able to provide. Kat will only provide what she can legally and morally provide and what she has proven."

Austin took the proffered papers, his eyes on Tag for a moment, lost in thought.

"So, she's part of the founding families. What does that actually mean?"

"That she has a trust fund coming to her. It was to go to her father but he's dead. They have not been able to confirm where she has been. A private investigator has been tracking her." Shay paused. "I wonder." His voice died away as he turned back to search the internet.

"Wonder what, Shay?" Brownie shared a look with the others. "Shay? What are you saying or thinking?"

"That the private investigator found them and has them safe, trying to work through what she has inherited. And from my reading, it's a lot." Shay was on his feet, heading for the printer. "Let me give you all this information. It explains it much better than I can."

Brownie frowned as his phone kept vibrating and he pulled it out, not knowing the number. He rose and headed for the hallway where he would have privacy, his eyes on the men working away in the office.

"Brownie? This is Jason Oates. You'll have come across my name, I think."

"Jason Oates? Yes. We just came across it." Brownie was puzzled why the investigator was reaching out to him and not Austin. "What do you want?"

"A chance to speak with you on your own. Only you. Rogan and Tate have asked for that. I'll call you with an address. But come on your own, please? Once you've met with me, then we'll talk with the others. This is the way it has to be. I'm sorry." The phone clicked off.

Brownie turned his phone over and over, staring at it as he did so. He didn't quite know how to tell the others. Tag stood beside him, a frown on his face.

"He called you?"

Brownie nodded, not quite sure how to respond.

"He did. He wants to meet with me only for now. But I need one of you with me. I'll push for that. Rogan and Tate sent him to me."

"I see." Tag's voice was low. "Let me go with you. Did he say when?"

"No. He didn't. I don't even know if they are still alive." Brownie's eyes raised to the office, not seeing it. "What else have you found out?"

"That Tate is in more danger than we thought. I can only pray that they are safe." Tag leaned against the cream painted wall of the hallway. "How do we find them, Brownie?"

"They'll be hiding in plain sight. That much I gather from what little he said. He really didn't say much." Brownie ran his hands through his hair.

"Let's get back to work and see what more we can
find out."

Chapter 38

Brownie paced the streets of the city, Tag keeping in step with him. He had set up a meeting with Jason Oates, adamant that Tag had to be involved. Jason had been agreeable, surprising Brownie but not Tag.

"Tag, we're here but where is he?" Brownie headed for an alleyway. "He said in here."

"He'll be watching us, just to ensure that we are on our own. And we are being followed." Tag looked around and then reached for a door, pulling it open and disappearing inside, Brownie following and snapping the lock closed as he did so. He could hear hurried footsteps outside and the door was pulled at but didn't open. He shared a look with Tag, who simply nodded.

Hearing soft sounds, Brownie and Tag spun, their eyes narrowed to squint through the dim lighting, brushing aside the dust and cobwebs in front of them. A figure appeared and then beckoned them to come with him. They exchanged glances and then with shrugs, followed the man to a stairway and up it to a room on the second floor of the building. They entered the door, surprised at how clean and tidy and well appointed the rooms were.

Jason Oates stood for a moment, watching them before he nodded.

"Thank you for coming, Brownie. Tag. Rogan was certain that you would not come on your own, Brownie. And I quite agreed with him. Tate wasn't sure." He pointed towards the table. "Sit. I have coffee here for you. Just let me grab my information and we'll talk."

Tag's hand was out to stop him, resting gently on Jason's arm.

"Are they alive and safe?"

"They are. I found them as they were being taken away and was able to get them free. They refused to come in, sending messages to their family that they were safe and alive but needed to stay in hiding for now. Reuben responded that he was aware of what was going on. Have you talked with him?"

"No, actually I haven't." Brownie frowned. "He's been avoiding us."

Jason grinned for a moment.

"He said he would. And it hasn't been hard for him to do so. He has assured me that his family is taking every precaution that they can to stay safe." He walked away into another room and then returned, dropping file folders onto the table and then reaching for his mug of coffee. He sat, his eyes drifting between the two men. "I know you two are Christians. Let's pray, okay? We need God's leading in how we proceed. This is when it gets very dangerous for the two."

Raising their heads thirty minutes later, Brownie just stared at Jason, who stared back. Neither man gave an inch. Tag watched, a slight smile on his face.

"Okay, you two. Let's get started. The sooner we get through this, the sooner Rogan and Tate can come home."

"Okay. Let's get started. Tate is related to the founding families or one of them. This has been hidden from her for years. She was not aware that her father had any connection to this town. She has simply said that her mother got rid of everything and wouldn't speak about him."

"That's correct. We have found that connection." Tag reached for the papers being shoved at him. "This is the proof?"

"It is. Rogan and Tate are aware of everything that I have discovered. You will need to provide it to Austin and have him verify it all. That I can't do for him."

Brownie read through the material and then read back through it. He then sat back, puzzled at how Jason had been able to find what they couldn't.

"I need to speak with Rogan and Tate. That is not an option." Brownie's eyes did not waver from Jason.

Jason nodded, knowing this would be the case.

"They thought this would be what you said. They are agreeable but not today. They want you to turn this in to Austin. Once they know that he has this information, then they will meet. But not in town. They are adamant that they won't meet in this town."

"Okay. So we come up with a place."

"We have a place arranged. It is not far from here and there will be security around them."

Tag stared at Jason.

"Abe."

Jason sighed. This was not to be known, he thought.

"Abe and his team. They'll make arrangements, get them there and then get you two there. They have another security team that is moving in to help."

Brownie nodded before he looked around.

"This is your place. I can tell."

"It is. I own this building. I don't do much with the bottom floor, leaving it open for whoever needs it. That gives me eyes and ears on the street when I need them. It is mutually beneficial to all of us."

"I can see that. Now, Tag, let's head out and see if we can find Austin. I think that he was in court today."

"That he was." Tag hesitated and then shook Jason's hand. "Keep us in the loop. You have our numbers. Use them."

"That I will. Thanks, fellows, for meeting with me." Jason nodded at the material. "That will keep you going for a while. I have more that I am working on. Whatever it is? It goes deep into the politics of this town."

"I am sure that it does." Brownie walked away from Jason, down the stairs and then out of the building, Tag following behind him.

Neither man spoke, neither sure what to say. That Rogan and Tate were alive and well was a relief. But the difficulty would be proving what they had been told, given how deep it seemed to run in the town.

"Can we do it, Tag?" Brownie wasn't confident that they could.

"We'll do our best, that's for sure. Austin should be home by now. Let's head that way."

Austin stared at the two men before pointing to his kitchen. He had had a long day in court, was tired and grumpy, and just wanted to relax. Only it didn't seem as if that would happen. Austin shot a glance at the clock and then reached for the casserole he had in the oven. They would eat and then talk.

"We met with Jason Oates today, Austin." Brownie stated simply what he needed to. "He's given us information for you that is very disturbing. This reaches well into the politics of our town."

Austin's movements stopped and he spun to stare at them.

"You did? Okay. Let's eat and then pray. Then you'll talk."

Chapter 39

Jason locked the door behind the two men and then stood, his hand resting against it. His head dropped. The secret was now out, where the couple was, and that worried him more than anything. He stepped away from the door, turning as he heard a door click and then soft footsteps. He stared at the couple standing hand in hand before him.

Rogan's hand tightened on Tate's, his eyes on Jason. They didn't move forward, just stood watching him. They both knew that this was dangerous for Jason. He had put himself out there for them, meeting with their two friends.

"Jason?"

Jason nodded before he moved to start a meal.

"Brownie and Tag have the information. They were to find Austin and pass it on." Jason turned, wiping his hands on a small towel that he threw over his shoulder. "They'll be in touch in the next day or so, I suspect."

"They will and so will Austin. He'll want in our meeting." Rogan rubbed at his face.

Tate shook her hand loose and moved to help Jason, her thoughts troubled.

"We need him to. That's not an option. Not at all." Tate placed the cutlery and then moved to make their coffee. She stood, back to the granite countertop, and stared at the two men. "We have to. He needs to be in on this. Jason, when do we go there? Rogan needs to be back with his people."

"He does. I spoke with the board chairman and he is aware that you two are safe. You have the complete confidence of the board. They want you to solve this and then come back."

"I see. I'm not sure that I will, given what we've gone through." Rogan seated Tate and then pulled out his own chair.

"That's fair." Jason asked the blessing on their food and then began to eat, watching as both Rogan and Tate picked at their meal. "You two need to eat."

"I know. It's just I have no appetite." Tate shoved her plate away after eating what she could. "Jason? How did you ever find us?"

"We do need to talk about that. We haven't." Jason rose to clear away their meal and refilled their coffee mugs. "Let's spend some time in prayer. God is here with you, but you need to feel His presence even more. Rogan, as a preacher, you understand that."

"I do but it's different when you're on the other side of the coin, as they say." Rogan's arm drew Tate close to him. "And with Tate involved, it's worse."

At last, Jason rose and went to retrieve his files. He set them down before he paced.

"Jason?" Tate's voice was worried.

"Okay. So we go back to how you were taken and who took you." Jason handed over a file. "This is the man responsible."

Rogan opened it, shock on his face.

"Him? I trusted him." He looked up, devastation on his face. "How? Why?"

"He's related to the board member who was removed. A cousin. He is aware that Tate has an inheritance coming to her. He wants it. Jake Twomey doesn't care how he gets it. He has money but never enough. He is involved in crime in this town, always has been, but keeps just under the radar and so far has avoided being arrested.

"His cousin, Tom Twomey, is the board member. I have evidence that he has always been into crime as well. He used his position to find those he could force into crime. There is relief in the shelter that he is gone.

"Now, your inheritance, Tate. It comes through your paternal side. One of your remote grandfathers was a founder of the town. It is not a large inheritance, something like a few million, and some buildings that are well rented. It has been waiting for you since you turned 18. The lawyers have been trying to track you and reached out to me. That's how I got involved."

"I see. All those years?" Tate wrapped her arms around herself, uncomfortable at having that much money. "I don't know what to say or do."

"Nothing at the present time, sweetheart. We'll meet with the lawyer and then make a decision." Rogan's arm tightened on her.

"Okay." Tate's head had turned as he spoke, before she leaned her head against his shoulder.

"Now, as to where you were taken?" Jason handed over another file. "This is where. A home that the Twomeys owned together. It is an opulent home. You were not maltreated, were you?" They shook their heads, not quite sure where he was heading with his comments. "They wanted to scare you, to have you sign documents that would turn over the inheritance. They then planned to remove you from the area."

"They did?" Tate turned to Rogan once more. "That's what he meant."

"Who?"

"The man who took us. He threatened us. I think it was when they had you in another room." Tate's hand tightened on Rogan's. "He said that there were plane tickets with our names on them and that we would be flown out of the country."

"He did? I wish I had heard him." Rogan had to tamp down his anger. "Jason?"

"That's what we're hearing. The street sources are coming forward, not to the police, but to myself. They feel that someone on the force is on the Twomeys' payroll. Only they're not sure who."

Tate nodded, her eyes on Rogan, who was staring at Jason, disbelief on his face.

"I have felt that, Jason. Those were the rumours that I heard. I'm sorry, Rogan."

Rogan shook his head, not quite sure what to say.

"It's okay." He rubbed at his face. "We need to talk with Austin, Jason, and now. We have to tell him what happened. Where can we meet that's safe?"

"Not here. That's not happening. It was dangerous enough to bring in Brownie and Tag. They said someone had followed them." Jason sat back, his fingers tapping on the wood table top.

"We can't disguise ourselves. Rogan's brace would give him away." Tate was on her feet, working to clean the kitchen and make a new pot of coffee.

Chapter 40

Austin turned from where he had been standing, contemplating the river. He had been asked to come here. He had frowned as he listened to Jason Oates ask that. Jason had hung up before he could ask why. He stared at the boat that had pulled to the shore and Jason had appeared, motioning him forward.

"Austin? Come one. Let's go." Jason searched the area, not feeling watched for a change.

"Jason? A boat?" Austin clambered aboard and sat, watching as Jason sped away from the shore as safely as he could.

"I'm taking you to Rogan and Tate."

That simple statement stopped Austin completely. He stared at Jason and then around.

"Where?"

"At a cabin. They're well and are wanting to tell their story." Jason pulled up to a dock and tied off the boat. "In here, Austin."

Austin walked through the door of the cabin, searching for Rogan and Tate but not seeing them. He turned, his eyes taking in the neatness of the rooms, feeling the heat from the wood fireplace that was needed on that cool, damp day.

"Jason? Where are they?"

"They're here. We're keeping them under cover for now. They were adamant that they would not appear until you were here and on your own." Jason stared at Austin. "There is a leak on your force."

"We thought that. We've found the woman responsible and are dealing with her. She's related to the Twomeys."

"She is. And who knows how many cases that she has tampered with as a crime scene tech."

"That's all well and good, but that doesn't bring much comfort." Rogan spoke from the kitchen area, where he and Tate were now standing.

"Rogan? I'm sorry. We didn't know." Austin stared at him, seeing the distress and change in his friends, not what he wanted to see or liked to see. "Now? Can we talk?"

"We can. Let's sit." Rogan pulled Tate over to the couch and down to a sitting position. He returned with a tray and set it on the table in front of them before he sat, staring hard at Austin.

Austin sighed to himself. This is not how he expected to find these two. Not at all. He knew that Brownie and Tag had seen them. They had been open with him, passing on the information as had been requested, but both had refused to tell him where they were.

"Okay, let's get started. And I want all the details. There have been many people looking for you." His voice was hard and tight, anger just below the surface, anger that he needed to ask God to remove.

Tate and Rogan shared a look, not quite sure where to start. Tate leaned against Rogan, her hand tight in his.

"Austin? You know about that inheritance I have?" Tate's voice was hesitant, causing Austin to frown at her. It didn't sound like her at all.

"I do. It's yours, that has been determined. So, how does this fit in?" Austin's pen was out as was his laptop, set to record their conversation. He looked between the two. "How be you go first, Rogan? And then Tate."

Rogan nodded.

"We can do that, I guess." He prayed hard, not feeling close to God at that point, but as a preacher, knowing that God was there with him. That not always would they feel the strong presence of their Heavenly Father but that there was no question that they were not alone.

"Okay. To go back to that day. We were awakened in the night by sounds outside the house. We got up, dressed, and then heard someone walking in the house. The security system was sounding. We climbed out of the bathroom window and headed for the house next door. We hid by the shed, not sure where to go.

"About five minutes after we had run from our home, I decided that we could move away. Only a man stood in front of me. Our hands were bound behind us. Then we were forced to walk towards the fields and through them towards the farm house. The man forced us into the drive shed there and we waited. A truck finally arrived and we were forced into it. Tate was in the front seat. They made me sit behind her. They didn't hold any weapons on us. That's the strange part.

"We were then taken to an older house just outside town. It's well taken care of and opulent. I have no idea who owns it. We were allowed freedom inside it but just couldn't go outside. We were well treated, which is strange." Rogan paused at that time to swallow a mouthful of coffee, trying to make sense of it all.

"We weren't asked anything. Not asked to provide any statements. Nothing. It's like they had just taken us to keep us safe. Does that even make sense?" Rogan stared at Austin, who stared back, his mind racing as to what had actually happened.

"We had photos taken of us and were told that they would be sent to you. They knew who you were."

Austin stared down at his notes. *They were not taken to harm them, now were they, Lord? They were taken to protect them. But from who and what? This changes the whole course of what I am looking at. And I don't think it's just about Tate's inheritance.*

Chapter 41

Tate began to speak, breaking into Austin's thoughts. He turned his look towards her, seeing the puzzlement and fear that she was feeling.

"Austin, Rogan's right. We were well treated. Just confined. It's not like we were prisoners. It never made sense. Jason found us. He said that he was given directions to where we were. Who does that? Jason just walked in and out with us."

Jason was nodding.

"That's exactly what happened. I received word from someone on the street that they were there. I headed there. The door was unlocked and I just opened it and walked in. They stood and stared at me and then headed out to my car. I took them to a safe place and they have been there since."

Austin was extremely puzzled. This was not a normal run-of-the-mill kidnapping.

"The men who took you? Were they around much?"

"Someone was with us all the time. They weren't armed, which they should have been if they were guards." Rogan was puzzled as well.

"They weren't? They weren't professionals then." Austin looked down at his notes, reaching to print their statements and having them read them and sign them. "This is not how we usually do this, but it will work for now."

Jason moved around, refilling their coffees, finding food for them. He had remained quiet, having a sense that Austin was troubled by what had happened.

"Your family, Rogan? Do they know?"

Rogan nodded, his hand tightening on Tate. This was something that they had discussed and Tate had been adamant that his family had to know that they were alive and well.

"They do. We made sure of that. We have taken steps to ensure their safety. If you look for them in this town, you will not find them. We have them hidden away."

Austin nodded, knowing that when the time was right, he would be told. Their resources were stretched thin. At the moment, Rogan's family had not been on the radar for being in harm's way but he knew only too well that they could and would be used to draw out Rogan and Tate.

"That's fine. I trust that you're correct. Now, what do we do with you two?"

"We had made arrangements to meet with you in a secure place well away from here. Things have changed. We have information that someone has put out a contract on Tate, to take her inheritance. But that is not the real reason we moved this forward. You have a leak, which you have acknowledged. That leak has threatened these two." Jason's look was hard as he stared back at Austin. "We can't wait for them to strike. We need to make plans and move towards bringing them in. If Rogan and Tate go public again, I can't guarantee their safety."

"No, we can't." Austin sat back, lost in thought, before he was on his feet, pacing. He thought better sometimes when he was in movement. He was a runner, his daily run a way to clear his mind and sort through what he was facing in a day.

"Austin? What do we do?" Tate's voice held a pleading tone to it.

"I'm not sure. You say Brownie and Tag were around?" He spun to catch their nods. "Okay, so were they to talk to the others?"

"Not that we know of, but they might. Austin? You'll need to process this without giving away what you've been told. How do you do that?" Rogan leaned forward, his hands rubbing at his face. "We need to find out what all this is about."

"Revenge." Tate's quiet voice and her statement brought the three men's looks towards her.

"Why that?" Austin sat once more, his gaze steady on her. He knew her well enough to know that she just didn't make statements that she hadn't thought through.

Tate shrugged, not quite sure how to express her thoughts.

"I didn't know about the inheritance. Has anyone talked to Mom to see what she says? You have said that she is in police protection."

"She is. And she has been asked. She denies knowing about it."

"I see." Tate slumped back on the couch, her arms crossed over her abdomen, a distressed look on her face. "I just don't understand how she could walk away as she did. I mean, I know that she was distant all my life but I thought that she loved me. Is she involved in this, after all?"

"That is one thing that we are looking at, Tate." Austin's voice and face had sympathy for the younger lady. "It takes time to track back through all the towns that she has lived in. And each one of those towns? They were the ones that you lived in. We stated this before. She was following you. As to the reason? She has not or will not say."

"Do I need to meet her face to face?" Tate looked up, not really wanting to do that.

"No, not at the moment. At some point? It is entirely possible that you will need to. Just to sort out what has happened and to bring a conclusion to what you've faced."

Rogan had been listening closely.

"Austin? What aren't you saying?" His eyes never left his bride.

"What am I not saying? That she is a suspect? At present, anyone who may have been involved with you two like this would be. You know that, Rogan. Now, what do we do with you two?"

Jason approached, handing over another pile of files.

"Take this, Austin. I'll take you back to where you left your car and you'll need to work through these. Keep it close to yourself. I still think there are others involved in the department.”

“I see. Well, we know that the Twomeys reach deep into politics and businesses in town.” Austin sighed, knowing that he had to speak with other departments. “I have to talk to others, Jason. This is much deeper and darker than just Rogan and Tate.”

“We know that and expect that. Just be cautious, that’s all we ask.” Jason shared a look with Rogan before he walked away, leaving Tate and Rogan staring at the door before staring at one another.

Chapter 42

Tate rose to pace, Rogan watching her closely, seeing how tense she was. They had not planned on meeting with Austin yet, and that put Tate out of her comfort zone, he knew.

"Tate? What are you thinking?"

Tate shrugged, turning to face him, her hands leaning on the kitchen countertop.

"I'm not sure, sweetheart. Something is still off and I have no idea what it is. Do you?"

"No, I don't. I know Austin is working his hardest to solve this. But you are correct. There is something off. Let's contact Shay or Storm."

"We can. Evan is another one to talk to. Doesn't he work for Emma?

"He does and my last email from her had lots of information that we still have to go through."

"Can we leave it for today? I'm just exhausted with all this." Tate slumped back down beside him, welcoming his arms around her and his kiss on her cheek.

"We can. Jason will be back late this afternoon, he said." Rogan settled back, content to hold his bride. "Let's spend the time in prayer. And here's your Bible. We need to go through the verses that

God has for us. This is when it gets dangerous, you know.”

“I do.” Tate grew quiet and then slept, her body unable to handle any more stress at the moment.

Rogan watched her and then his eyes grew heavy as well. He too slept, not knowing that in the next couple of days, their lives would be in grave danger and that they would be separated, each convinced the other was dead.

Late that afternoon, Jason appeared, a bag of food in his hand. He searched for the couple, not finding them. Then he heard Tate’s voice, a bit of laughter in it, as he reached for the back door. Opening it, he found Tate and Rogan facing one another across the pile of logs that lay near the back door.

“Okay, you two. I have food.” Jason grinned at them, causing them to spin towards him.

“Food? Did you say food?” Tate almost ran past him. “He’s not getting any.”

Rogan gave a laugh as he walked towards Jason.

“You said the magic words, my friend. She searched the cupboards earlier, not liking just the canned and boxed foods that she found.”

Jason began to laugh.

“Then, I guess I did right.” His hand stopped Rogan for a moment. “Listen, how are you two really doing?”

Rogan shrugged, his eyes on Tate who stood watching him from the kitchen even as her hands unpacked the food.

"As well as we can, I guess. It's been hard on her. The way we married? It shouldn't have been that way but it was. I love her more than anything or anyone other than God. I need to keep her safe. Only I don't know how to."

"We get that, Rogan. I had a long talk with Austin. He wants to bring you two in and hide you somewhere."

"I gathered that he would. Only that doesn't seem possible, does it?"

Late that night, Tate raised her head from where she had curled up on the couch. She had been restless and reluctant to go to bed. Rogan had nodded and simply sat in a chair near her, a blanket covering him. She heard Jason's voice raised in anger and then fear, calling at them to run.

Rogan was on his feet, reaching for Tate, pulling her from the cabin. They ran for the woods surrounding the cabin, not sure where to go. Tate's feet tangled in the debris on the trail and she tumbled to the ground, taking Rogan with her. Before they could regain their footsteps, hard grasps hauled them to their feet and then shoved them along the pathway.

Tate's breath came in gasps as she struggled to control her sobs. Rogan stumbled as he tried to keep to his own feet. This was not what was to have happened, he thought. Not at all. They were to have gotten away and stayed safe. *God, where are You?*

Tate struggled against the hands that were holding her, shoving her into a vehicle. She twisted on the seat, trying to find Rogan, not seeing him in the vehicle.

"Rogan? Where is he?" Her words spat at her captor.

He simply gave a cruel laugh.

"He's not coming with you. Not this time. This time you are on your own."

She twisted once more, to stare out the back window of the truck, not seeing Rogan or another vehicle.

"Please? Where is he? I need to be with him."

"Not happening. Not this time. This time, you're with us and not him. And you won't be with him. Not ever again." He gave a cruel laugh as she stared at him, her mouth opening and closing.

Tate slumped back, her hands now handcuffed in front of her. This can't be happening, she thought. Not now. Not when we were so close to getting whoever it was.

Rogan rolled to his side, a hand to his head, before he pulled it away, feeling the stickiness of the blood on it. He sat gingerly up, not quite aware of what was happening before he clambered to his feet, a hand out to rest against a nearby tree to balance himself. He struggled to walk, heading back to where the cabin was he thought. His blurry eyes sought the cabin and he stumbled towards it, his hand hitting the door and shoving it open. He sought to find Tate, not finding her. Despair raised within him as he didn't see her. A figure sprawled on the floor caught his attention. Rogan dropped to his knees, his shaking hand reached out to touch it. Jason, he thought. He is alive but where is Tate? He spun on his knees, not seeing her. His body crumpled forward as despair and terror for his bride surged through him.

Chapter 43

Austin walked the perimeter of the yard, searching for any clues. Rogan had found his phone and managed to call for help. He was disturbed beyond belief that Tate had disappeared again, this time on her own, and that shouldn't have happened. Somehow or other, they had been tracked. He had talked to his supervisor and also the police chief, who were not surprised at what he had discovered. They had had the same thoughts and had brought in an outside force to probe that very thought. He turned as Rogan approached, a hand out to stay him.

"Austin? What happened?" Rogan's voice was broken, pain evident as well as his worry about his bride.

"Someone sold us out. That's what happened." Austin's voice was brittle, anger spewing with his words.

"In the department. But who and why?" Rogan kicked at a rock in his path, sending it flying across the ground. He heard the night critters scattering as it landed across the clearing.

"We know who. The why is what we're working on. She was being arrested as we got word about this. Unfortunately, we need to find the ones who hired her. And that is a work in progress. We are closer than we were. Your friends' work and that of Emma and her group have definitely helped.

We're almost there, Rogan. I know that's no consolation for you." Austin turned him around, a hand on his shoulder directing him back to the cabin. "Let the paramedics assess you. Jason is on his way in to the hospital."

"How bad was he hurt?" Rogan slumped on a chair, not paying any mind to the hands that were checking him out.

"He's was still out when he left. He took a hard blow to his head." Austin moved away to speak with one of the officers, standing so that he could watch Rogan. "We need to get him back to town, George."

"We do. Only he's not going to want to go. Not with Tate missing out here."

"I would say that she's already been moved from here. That's what I would do."

"That's what they expect us to do. I would say otherwise." George was an older officer, street wise from working the streets all his patrol life. "They'll stay in this area and watch what's happening."

Austin pursed his lips as he thought that through, his eyes on the night sky, watching the clouds scud across the moon and stars. He could hear the night sounds in his ears, wishing it was different, that he was out here to relax and not investigate the abduction of a friend.

"That's true." Austin sighed again. "Tell you what. You decide who you want to work with you and start going from cabin to cabin. There is also a campground near here." Austin rubbed at his face. "This is going to take a long time."

"It might. But then, we know who we're looking for." George grinned as he held up his phone. "Daniel and Brownie have come through. They have addresses here for us to look at."

"They're ahead of us. Of course, Brownie would have been, given that they met with Rogan and Tate."

"They did? I wondered. Brownie wanted to say something, I think, but wouldn't."

Rogan looked up through bleary eyes, not quite focusing on Austin.

"Austin? Have you found her?"

"Not yet but we're looking." Austin shared a look with the paramedics and nodded at them. "Rogan, they'll take you in and have you seen at Emergency. And then officers will take you home and stay with you. We'll find Tate and bring her home."

Rogan paced his home early the next morning. He had been assessed, a bandage slapped on the cut on his head, and then he was sent home. He had refused to fill the pain medication prescription, not wanting that feeling of not being aware of what was going on. Officers were in the house with him and also patrolling outside, a patrol car in his driveway.

He turned as he heard footsteps and saw his father approaching him, reaching to draw him into a father hug that tightened as sobs shook Rogan's body.

"Son? Any word?" Reuben's voice was low. He felt Rogan's head shaking against him. His heart was breaking for his son even as he prayed for him.

———

"They don't know where she is. Austin said they were looking." Rogan stepped back, swiping at his face, trying to hide the traces of his emotions. He bent to pick up the little calico kitten that Tate had discovered hiding in their yard one day and cuddled her close to him. "Mom? Reece? Rori?"

"They're on their way here. Austin has asked that we be kept together. That's what we have been pushing for." Reuben reached to hug his son again before he reached past him to pull a chair out and shove him down. "Have you taken anything for that headache?"

"I won't." Rogan rubbed at the table, not quite sure how he was to feel or act. He had never been in this position before. And right now, he doubted that God was there or even heard his prayers. He doubted his calling as a minister, feeling his humanness greatly at that point.

Reuben nodded, his eyes rising to where he heard more footsteps and then walked to gather his family close to him. Rogan's mother was away from her husband and then gathering her son close to her, a mother's arms trying to comfort her adult son as best she could. She had no idea just how he felt. She couldn't, not having been in such a situation as this.

"Mom? Should you be here?"

"We have to be, son. This is where they want us. Together."

Rogan nodded, his eyes on his brother and his sister, seeing their fear and the concern that they were feeling. He nodded slowly before Rori rushed to hug him and then moved away, pacing the living room.

Reece simply leaned against a door frame, his phone out as he read an email before passing his phone to Rogan.

Rogan frowned as he did so, reading the email. He looked up, hope on his face. Abe had been in touch, with word that they were on their way towards Rogan and Tate. He didn't say why, but Rogan was trying to read between the lines. He hoped that Abe knew where Tate was and that he would rescue her.

Chapter 44

Tate roamed the room that she was locked into. She had not been taken that far from the cabin but it was far enough that she knew she couldn't make it back there. It was night, for one thing, and for another thing, her sneakers had been roughly pulled from her feet, leaving her barefoot. Tate knew that wouldn't stop her if she could manage to get away.

She searched the room and the small ensuite, looking for anything she could use to defend herself. There was nothing. She walked to the door, a hand on the knob, an ear pressed to it. She could hear the faint sound of conversation and could smell the coffee that the men had made. Tate had not been threatened with words but she knew that was implied. She had fought them when she was pulled from the truck and again as she was shoved into the room and the door slammed and locked behind her.

The window drew her attention. Tate studied it, seeing that it wasn't nailed closed. She shot a look behind her, desperate to escape, worried about Jason but more than beyond herself worried about Rogan. Tracks streaked her cheeks from the tears that she had wept and she swiped angrily at the stickiness. Her fingers felt for a lock and didn't find out. Tate frowned. This was so bizarre, she thought. The door was locked, but not the window? She cautiously leaned on the upper portion of the bottom window, sliding it upwards. When there was enough space that she could wiggle her way through, she went out feet first, landing on the softness of the grass that had grown right to the wall. The window closed behind her, Tate crept on silent feet towards the woods, finding a path that she could follow.

Standing in the shadows and darkness, Tate stared behind her. That didn't just happen, did it, Lord? Did I really just get away? Did You provide that for me? If so, thank you.

Tate almost ran along the path, not sure where she was heading but knowing that she was heading away from the cabin and towards safety or so she prayed. She didn't know the area, didn't know if she was heading for a road, the lake, or into more danger. She slid to a stop as a figure rose in front of her, a scream rising from her.

The figure simply reached for her hand and pulled her with him, before his companion pointed silently to her feet. An exclamation came from him and he swept Tate up into his arms, a squeak coming from her. They rushed from the area, heading for a large black SUV. Tate was wrapped into a blanket and then deposited gently on a seat. She could hear quiet conversation through the open door before the men were beside her, the doors closed, and the vehicle moved away.

Micah studied Tate, seeing the ravages on her face of what she had just been through. He shared a look with Joseph and Luke and then with Murphy. He knew Abe and their other three teammates were near the cabin where Tate had been held. They were in contact with Austin and had police officers moving in to make arrests. How she had been able to escape? That was a question they would deal with.

Murphy turned in his seat, his eyes once more on Tate, before he spoke.

"Tate?" Murphy patiently waited while Tate processed his voice and realized she knew him. "Tate? Did they hurt you?"

Tate shook her head, her emotions leaving her unable to speak for a moment.

"No, they didn't. Not physically. Mentally and emotionally? They did." She blinked rapidly, unable to control her emotions for a moment. "Rogan?"

"He's fine. He was hit over the head but he was able to call for help. Jason was hurt but he's under treatment." He watched with compassion as Tate's eyes slid closed and tears trickled down her face. Luke simply handed her a handkerchief.

"Thank you." Her voice was barely audible. "I want to go home."

"And that's where we'll take you. Austin will meet us there." Murphy nodded as Tate slumped back on the seat and her eyes closed as she slept, her emotions draining any stamina that she had left.

Joseph reached for Tate's hand and pulled her from the vehicle, leading her towards the house. Her steps were stumbling as she tried to awaken but was not sure if she even could. Rogan turned as he heard more footsteps, his arm resting on the back of his chair before he was on his feet, reaching for Tate. She stiffened for a moment until she recognized his voice and then collapsed against him, sobs shaking her body. The men blinked rapidly, turning away to cover their own emotions.

Reuben approached his son, his arms around the couple, his prayer reaching through to Tate, who looked up, a tremulous smile on her face. She was home but now they had to find who was responsible and bring them to justice.

Austin finally approached the home, fatigue weighing down his steps. They had been over to the cabin, arresting the men, catching them totally unaware. Their shock when they were told that their captive had escaped was almost amusing, Austin thought, if it hadn't been so life threatening for Tate and Rogan. He looked for the couple, not finding them.

"They're sleeping, Austin." Reece spoke from the front porch. "We sent them to bed. They were almost asleep on their feet. Your boss was around and took Tate's statement. He said that you were tied up on an investigation or something like that."

"I was. Abe around?"

Reece shook his head.

"No, they had to head out. Something about a training session that they had booked for today."

Austin nodded, a yawn catching him unawares.

Reece's hand was out to draw Austin into the house.

"You're almost asleep on your feet. The couch is free. Grab some sleep and start fresh later this morning. Your boss told us to make sure that you got some sleep."

Austin nodded, his eyes already closing as he settled down to sleep. His friends were free and safe for now. They were working on the search and arrest warrants that were needed. He would be up and on his feet in a few hours, ready to be part of that. Only, he was afraid that they were missing something really big and important and that was not what he wanted to think.

Chapter 45

Tate roused in the morning, her senses telling her she was safe. She felt Rogan's arm around her and snuggled closer, seeking comfort from him. Rogan was awake as well, his heart heavy for his bride but raised in praise that they were both home.

"Tate? What happened?"

"Abe. Some of his men found me. I was able to get out of the room I was locked in. The window opened and I could jump out. I don't know that the men were even aware that I had." She shifted her position so that she could see his face, seeing the bandage on the side of his head. "You're hurt."

"Not bad. Not like I could be. God protected us both and Jason as well. Jason was knocked out and was still unconscious as he was brought in. He'll be okay from what I understand."

"I'm so glad. I was so worried about both of you." She grew silent, just watching him. "What happens now?"

"Now? I was told that they're at the point in the investigation that they can start making arrests up the ladder towards the Twomeys. Only, Brownie let it slip that the Twomeys have gone into hiding."

"That's not what I wanted to hear." Tate drew a deep breath. "Okay, my preacher groom. What is God teaching us through this?"

"What is He teaching us? To trust Him. To lean on Him and not ourselves. To be a witness to those who are involved in all this. That's what Storm and Dougal both said. That they were used to be a witness to God through it all."

"I can see that." Tate shifted once more and then was on her feet. "Do you know how late it is?"

"I know. They let us sleep. Mom and Dad are here as are Reece and Rori." He too rose.

Tate nodded as she grabbed clean clothes and headed for the shower.

"I figured that they would be. I'll be really quick and then let you have the shower."

"Don't rush." Rogan grinned as the door shut quietly on his words. He knew that she would, just because that was Tate. He emerged from his own shower to find Tate sitting on the side of the bed, her arms wrapped around herself, a woebegone look on her face. "Tate? Sweetheart? What's wrong?" He simply gathered her close to his heart.

"Is this over yet, Rogan? Is it? I can't go on any more. Too many lives have been affected. Do they really think that by getting to me, they'll get to you and shut down the shelter and the mission?" She looked up at him as his arms tightened around her but he didn't speak.

Rogan stared down at her upturned face before he reached to kiss her. His head then rested against her. *Lord, she's suffering, thinking that she's the cause of it all. But that has never felt right. I think she's on to something here.*

"I don't know if they considered that. If they have, they have not told me." He was on his feet and moving towards the door. "Come on. Let's eat and then gather our friends."

"Sure. Why not?" Tate moved away from him, slowness in her steps, the very picture of defeat. It broke Rogan's heart to see that.

Tate stood in the hallway, listening to men's voices with the occasional comment from a lady. Our home is full, she thought, but with who? Rogan reached for her hand, tugging her forward, to stand in the hallway as well, staring at his friends who had gathered as well as the board members.

"Rogan? Tate? You're awake and on your feet." Reuben moved to hug them both. "Mom has gone out for a bit, a meeting that she had to be at, with Rori and Reece. The rest of the gang is all here, as we say."

"So I see." Rogan moved among his friends, greeting them, the ladies extending hugs to him before they surrounded Tate.

An hour later, Rogan stood in his office, watching as Austin worked away, Brownie and Daniel working with him, his other friends having found chairs or seats on the floor to do the same. Abe's men moved among them inside and outside the house, vigilant, knowing that this might just be the time that something drastic and devastating happened.

Tate was with the ladies and the board members, spending time in prayer. She raised her head at last, staring at the board chairman who was watching her

"Tate?" The man's look was kindly. Joseph Atkins had known Rogan all of his life and loved him as a son. To have had Rogan and his bride face what they had? That had consumed him in trying to solve it.

"Joseph? I have a question but I'm not sure if it has been asked or answered. It has never made sense that someone would go after me. Not at all. I mean, I know I'm to have an inheritance coming to me that I never knew about. But what if this was all staged with me, including the inheritance, to get to Rogan and through Rogan to the shelter and mission? To close them down. What would happen to the people if that was the case?"

Joseph looked down for a moment, his head nodding at her words. She had gone right to the heart of it, he thought, while the rest of us has struggled to find the reason.

"You are correct in your suppositions, Tate. That is what the investigation is now showing. Someone wants to shut us down and then level the buildings. The property is worth millions in development and that is before any building is done. Austin is working on that premise right now. We can't explain it all, but he is going to speak with you both as soon as he has sorted it out. My understanding is that the illegal gangs are involved in this."

"Money laundering." Tate sighed, her eyes raised to the ceiling. "Can we prove this?"

"We can." Austin stood near her, papers in his hand, watching her closely. "We have proved it,

Tate. Just a couple of days until we can make the arrests and then we'll meet." He walked away, leaving Tate staring after him, her mouth open.

Rogan walked towards her, taking Breckon's place beside his bride.

"It's almost over, sweetheart. Then, we can live our lives that God has planned." His eyes closed as he struggled with his emotions.

Tate sighed as well, her head on his shoulder, her eyes on Joseph.

"But who all on the board were involved?"

"Just the one person. Who is not related to your father after all. Even Emma has dug up that information. It was well hidden." Evan stood near them. "I'm sorry, Tate. Rogan. This should have been available to us but it was so well hidden that it has taken time for us to dig through all the levels. Someone went to a lot of work to hide it."

"And frame me? Is that what you're not saying?"

"Unfortunately, that may be the case. We're working it through."

Chapter 46

A week later, Rogan turned to Tate, reaching for the tray of food that she had just lifted and set it down. He wrapped her in his arm, kissing her thoroughly before leaning back and watching her. She was still under a lot of stress, not having all the answers that they should have had. Their friends and family had gathered that day, with a promise that they would find out the answers. Only Tate had maintained that there was still someone out there. Someone who wanted Rogan dead. How she had come up with that, she just wasn't sure. And she just couldn't explain it away either. Austin had simply shaken his head, stated that they had everyone, and why would she think that?

"I'm sure there is someone else. I don't think that Austin believes me."

Rogan nodded.

"He thinks that he has everyone. But I agree with you. So do the guys. Emma is still searching, even with Abe and his guys and their ladies here. Our backyard is almost not big enough."

Tate smiled, knowing that they had quite a crowd in the yard. Their neighbours were involved as well and had willingly set up tables and chairs for the overflow. Rogan had been a wonderful neighbour over the years, willing to help or just listen as the case might be. They were just ready to have this all over for him and his beloved bride.

Emma approached the couple, Kat with her, papers in their hands, a disturbed look on her face. She had found out more information that was verified but she wasn't quite sure how to approach either one.

Rogan looked at Emma, looked at Kat, and then looked up at the blue of the sky, watching fluffy white clouds and the circling of the birds. She has information for us, he thought.

"Emma? What did you discover?" He reached for the paperwork.

"It's what we thought at the beginning and then set aside." Emma stared down at the papers. "It was to go after you, Rogan, all along. Tate was incidental to it all. If you hadn't married her, they would have found someone for you to marry. They are planning on playing that you are not fit to be a minister, have mental health issues, and that both of you are involved in the criminal aspect of what they're doing. We have documentation that they have tried to file, but the mission and shelter lawyers have prevented that. I talked to them before and warned them to watch for this."

"So then, what it is really about?" Tate was puzzled, her eyes on Austin as he stood beside Emma.

"To bring down the mission and shelter, Rogan, Tate. They want the land and this is the only way that they could do that. If they made it appear that you two were dishonest, involved in crime, and were hiding it, then they would sue the mission and shelter, have a judge disband the board, and shut down both.

They have been in the planning for a long time. The Twomeys were their henchmen as we say to all this."

"They were? I see." Tate paced away and then was back, her hand gripping Rogan's outstretched one. "How do we fight back?"

"That is what we need to talk about." Kat spoke up, her eyes on Emma. "We have come up with a plan, but it is dangerous. Abe and our guys will be your security as we do that." She spoke quickly, Emma nodding, the other three just staring at her in disbelief.

"We do what?" Tate's voice rose in disbelief before she clapped her lips closed. "They'll never believe that."

"But they will. They will think that they have driven a wedge between you two and that you don't want to stay married to a preacher. That it's just too much in the public eye and too stressful for you." Kat grinned. "We'll make it seem so real that they will believe us."

"Okay. So when?" Rogan looked past Emma to see Abe and Murphy standing there, ready to help in the plans.

Abe nodded as he heard the plans. The men on his team had met and discussed something like this, knowing how Emma thought. They knew the risk involved but were certain that both Rogan and Tate were ready to take that step.

"We need to keep it between us, though." Abe spoke up. "Austin? Can you clear that with your supervisor and police chief?"

"I can. We've been tossing scenarios around and this was one thing that we considered and then set on the back burner." He looked around. "Let's enjoy today, meet tonight to finalize plans, and then start the story going around tomorrow. Rogan and Tate? You're both sure?"

Rogan wrapped an arm around Tate, his eyes on her face as she looked up at him, lost for a moment in the look of love and complete trust in him that showed in her eyes.

"We are. Let's party today and then start the campaign to bring down the mob."

Chapter 47

Rogan stared at Tate the next morning outside of the shelter building, his face kept neutral, but his heart breaking for her. She stood back from him, her arms folded across her abdomen, not looking directly at him. *This is hard,* he thought. *We talked about it, made plans, prayed over it, but we are still not sure if this is the correct way to do this. Our families will be floored and more than upset with us.*

"Tate? Just what are you saying?" Rogan's voice was pitched at a level that Abe and his men could hear him. He knew that others were around, including those who they suspected. He had called the newspaper the day before and the radio station, just to say that he was returning to the shelter and mission with the board's blessing. Enough time had been lost to whatever it was that they had faced.

"That I think we made a mistake. That we shouldn't have married." Tate blinked rapidly, knowing that what she was saying had been discussed between them many times in private, but this time, it was different. This time? They were putting it out there for the whole town to hear and see. She stepped back as Rogan reached for her. "No, Rogan. I can't do this. I need to move on and to another town." Tears blinded her eyes as she turned and ran, heading for shelter and those of Abe's men who waited for her, to whisk her away to safety.

Rogan stood, his hand still outstretched, not quite believing that Tate had actually run from him. Distress and devastation showed on his face before his hand dropped as did his head. He turned slowly, heading for his office, to shut the door behind him and sink down in his chair. *This was just too real,* he thought. *Please, Lord? Let this end today.*

A knock at his door roused him from his work around the lunch hour. He called for the person to enter and then froze as he saw who it was. Emma was right, he thought. They really are here in town.

"Rogan!" Amos Maguire stared at Rogan, a gloating expression on his face. He threw a number of papers on Rogan's desk. "I hear tell that your wife walked away from you. Tsk! Tsk! Can't even keep your bride in your life! Now that she's gone, let's come to an agreement.

"An agreement? What would that be?" Rogan had reached for the sensor on his belt, touching it and activating the microphone that Micah had rigged up for him. Austin had cleared it with a judge the night before so it would be admissible as evidence.

"An agreement. You're done here as the preacher. We'll see that your name is drawn through the mud. You have mental issues that need to be dealt with. You will resign from here and enter a mental health institute. Your little scene with your wife will aid in your admission to there. Then, we go after the board and send them that way as well. The shelter and the mission will be closed as of today. We're buying the land." Maguire sneered at the look on Rogan's face. "And your wife? She'll be removed from this town and sent somewhere she'll never be seen again."

Rogan was on his feet, fists clenched at his sides at Maguire gave an evil grin. He threw himself at the older, heavyweight man, his fist connecting with the man's jaw. Maguire stumbled backwards even as one of his bodyguards slammed his pistol butt only Rogan's head and shoulder, sending the younger man to the floor. Rogan's body sprawled lifelessly at Maguire's feet.

Maguire stared dispassionately down at Rogan before he shrugged his suit coat back into place and moved to walk from the room. The bodyguard had backed away, into the hallway of the building before he stopped, feeling the barrel of a weapon in his back and then handcuffs around his wrists. Maguire stared back at Rogan before he too left the room, not seeing the men now surrounding him.

"So, Michael. Let's head for the courts and file our paperwork." Maguire waited, not hearing Michael respond promptly as he always required his help to do. "Did you hear me?" His voice rose in anger before he felt a hand on his arm and then handcuffs around his own wrists. "What is the meaning of this? Let me go! I will have your jobs for this!"

"Not this time, Maguire." Austin shoved the older man ahead of him, disgust evident on his face for a moment. "This time we have you right where we have wanted you for years. The only place that you are going is to jail and then to face the courts yourself."

"I want a lawyer. And I will have your jobs."

"Not likely on the last. And of course you want a lawyer. Only he won't help you get away this time."

The paramedics moved in at that point, brushing past the men, to find Rogan on his feet and in pain. He shook off the suggestion that he needed to go to Emergency. stating that he only wanted to find his bride. He heard running footsteps at that point, turning slightly, almost going back to the floor as Tate's body hit his hard.

Abe stood and watched the couple. Another successful arrest, he thought. We just need to watch these two for the next few days and then we can walk away. His eyes raised to the ceiling as he breathed a prayer of thankfulness. He had no idea what this couple had learned through their experience but he knew that each one who went through something like this grew closer to their Heavenly Father and was more fit to minister to others.

Chapter 48

Two weeks after his showdown with Maguire, Rogan stood shoulder to shoulder with Reece in his backyard. Family and friends had once more gathered, this time just to celebrate that their adventure was over. His eyes found Tate, seated between his mother and Rori, laughter sparkling on her face. Now that they were no longer in danger, her spirit and personality were sparkling forth. He was so grateful and thankful that neither one of them had faced the life and death situations that their friends had. What they had faced though? It had drawn them closer together as a couple and closer to their Heavenly Father.

Tate looked up at that point, her smile huge as she found him watching her. She was content, she thought, happy, loved by a wonderful man, and finding the family and friends that she had so longed for. She had spoken with her mother but neither one of them was ready to meet face to face. Tate had a lot to work through in that relationship and just didn't know if she could ever face the lady who had given birth to her.

Rori was watching Tate and then Rogan, a smile on her own face.

"You know, Tate, I have never seen Rogan happier. He is so in love with you."

Tate blushed even as she nodded.

———

228

"He is. He is a wonderful compassionate man who cares deeply for his family but also for those around him. That makes him the preacher that he is. He models our Lord's example each and every day."

Reuben spoke up at that point, his eyes shifting between the couple.

"Did everything get sorted out at last?"

Austin spoke from where he was perched on the porch railing, a freedom in his words that had not been there previously.

"As much as we can. It's still an open investigation as it now involves other jurisdictions. The prosecutors are working with us in refining the charges. And there are many. The Twomeys were lackies for Maguire. He wanted the land to build, using laundered money to do so. We have arrested those in the politics and businesses in this town who were involved. Not as many as we thought but there was a number."

"And the leak on the force?" Tate shared a look with Rogan as he took Rori's spot beside her, an arm drawing her close.

"We found all of them. A patrol officer. An administrative secretary. A crime scene tech. A detective." Austin was saddened at that. Good people brought down by greed. "We have to go back over all the cases that they were involved in and that makes a lot of work for us." He suddenly grinned. "But I hear that the mission and shelter are having a celebration."

"We are, Austin. A reach out to the community as a thank you for their support over this difficult time

———

and over all the years. That support has made us what we are today." Rogan grew thoughtful. "When I came on board as the minister for the mission, I didn't expect to help with the shelter. That just seemed to evolve over time. I have met many wonderful people who are down on their luck and just need a hand up, an ear to listen, a voice to speak for them, and a shoulder sometimes to cry on. That is what our aim is from now on. To strengthen that and to bring people on board who can help in that way."

"That's a wonderful way of looking at services, son." Reuben grew pensive. "What you two have gone through strengthens that in you both. Rogan, you are a son that your mother and I are proud of. Tate, you are exactly the helpmeet that he needs. Your experience over your lifetime gives you an understanding of what he faces in his work that not many have. I just thank God that you two were not more seriously injured."

Late that evening, Rogan looked up from the swing as Tate handed him a fresh mug of coffee and set hers on the table beside him. She curled up tight to him, his hug a welcoming and comforting embrace.

"Rogan? Would you have married at all?" Tate was hesitant to ask.

"Would I have married? I was waiting for you, sweetheart. I was simply waiting for you to walk into my life and heart. God planned this from before time began." He kissed her and then sat in silence.

"Okay. I see that." Tate stared up at him, his face in shadows with only the light of the solar lamps and the moon and stars to illuminate it. "Someone

asked me that today. I didn't know what to say other
than you were the other half of my heart."

Rogan was on a mission, no pun intended, as he searched the mission building and then the shelter. Tate was nowhere to be found. And she had been adamant that she would be there today. He spun and then grinned, snapping his fingers. He headed for the new playground that had been donated and stopped, his eyes on his bride of six months. A smile covered his face as he watched her sitting on the ground, surrounded by toddlers. Tate had taken over a playtime for them, to give the moms and dads a chance to attend classes, search for work, and see physicians or counsellors as they needed to. Her assistance was always so welcome, he thought. She didn't intrude or force her way into anything, just stood and watched and stepped in as she felt led to.

Tate looked up as Rogan dropped to the ground behind the toddlers, her smile widening at his grin. She finished her story, accepting the hugs and kisses the children lavished on her and then sat, resting back on her hands, her face tilting up to the late autumn sun.

"Tate? Have I told you today that I love and appreciate you so much?" Rogan's voice was low, only loud enough that Tate could hear him.

She looked over at him, a smile just for him on her face.

"You have. And I love you too. Now, what are you up to?" She took his hand as he reached to help her to her feet.

"Just wanting to spend time with my bride. I have been told to take someone out to lunch and for a walk along the riverbank and not to come back until Sunday. That's almost four days that we are free."

"It is? Oh, wonderful." She reached to hug him. "Let's grab some lunch and find our bench."

Later that afternoon, Rogan looked down at the head on his shoulder. Something was up with his bride but he wasn't sure what and she had not been sharing.

"Everything okay, sweetheart?"

Tate nodded, her thoughts muddled.

"It is. I am so thankful for your family and our friends. I don't think Mom and I will ever be close. She has said that she really doesn't want that. And that the inheritance I was to get? That was just a cover someone made up to try and separate us."

"Austin talked to you? He had hinted at that." Rogan grew pensive. "We'll manage without it. It's not like we ever had it. On a different note, are you happy just volunteering for those hours at the shelter?"

"I am. Those children are so wonderful. I just love their honesty and openness. And I am providing what their parents need as they work to get their lives back together." Tate grew silent for a moment. "We talked about a family at some point, sweetheart."

"We did but only when God thought that we were ready." His eyes were on her as she stared across the river. "Tate? Something you want to tell me?"

Tate sighed, her eyes coming to meet his.

"I guess God has decided that we're ready. We will be parents in the late winter, Rogan." She was hugged in a tight embrace, tears on both of their faces. "Rogan? Sweetheart? I do need to breathe."

Rogan loosened his arms slightly and grinned down at her.

"You will be the best mother ever. Can we keep our secret for now?"

Tate laughed at his nonsense, knowing in her heart that she felt the same.

"For now. But at some point, we will need to tell them. Please, Rogan? Pray for us and our little one."

Dear Readers:

Thank you for picking up the story of The Preacher, the tale of Rogan and his beloved lady, Tate. Once more these two characters have driven the story, with Tate throwing in a wrinkle near the end of the book. My characters are unruly at times and love to do this.

What Tate faced? Moving from town to town, uncertainty in what she wanted and faced? We all go through times of uncertainly, of wavering, of fear, of not trusting God as we should. That is our humanness coming through loud and clear. But trust this. God has promised never to leave us with His Comforter, the Holy Spirit. He has also promised never to leave us or forsake us. We were prayed for in the Garden. I cling to those verses when I face difficulties. We are also sheltered in His hands and in His care.

So, characters from the past have once more entered the story. Abe's team is found in the *His Guardians* series. Noah story is found in *His Warriors*. Rylee and Dave's story is *A Touch of His Garment*. Four of Rogan's friends are in *His Dreamseekers*. Two of them are in the first two books of *His Searchers*. I love revisiting with past characters who are beloved. They add to the story, moving it along if it seems to stall at all.

God bless each one of you on your journey with Him.

Ronna

www.ingramcontent.com/pod-product-compliance
Lightning Source LLC
Chambersburg PA
CBHW070457200726

48293CB00007B/2252